DECEMBER 16

JOY

CHRISTMAS ON EMERALD MOUNTAIN

CARA MALONE

LISBON PRESS

Copyright © 2017 by Cara Malone

All rights reserved.

No part of this book may be reproduced in any form or by any electronic or mechanical means, including information storage and retrieval systems, without written permission from the author, except for the use of brief quotations in a book review.

Previously published as *That Old Emerald Mountain Magic* by Cara Malone

ONE

JOY

Joy Turner could feel tears forming in the back of her throat. She wasn't the crying type, though, so she swallowed hard and pressed her lips into a thin smile as she pulled her best friend, Danny, into a hug.

"You're going to do great," she said over his shoulder as she made sure the tears would stay at bay before releasing the embrace. "They're gonna love you."

"Yeah?" he asked with a nervous smile. "What makes you so sure?"

"You've been playing the guitar since you were twelve years old," she said, then she rolled her eyes and teased him with, "and you make me listen to you practice every damn night so I know how good you are. Anyway, they wouldn't have called you if they didn't know exactly how awesome you are."

Two nights ago, Joy had been in the middle of brushing her teeth for bed when Danny appeared in the bathroom doorway with the biggest grin on his face, telling her that the front man for The Hero's Journey had just called and told him to get his butt to Memphis to fill an emergency vacancy. He'd auditioned to join the band six months earlier and been passed over, but they'd just had to fire a guitarist mid-tour and now they wanted Danny.

He hadn't hesitated to quit his restaurant serving job in town and start packing his bags, and Joy knew that this could be Danny's big break. Still, she felt a certain amount of foreboding as she saw him off. Danny was her oldest friend, and one of the few that had remained in their little resort town of Emerald Hill after high school was over. Denver was less than an hour away and it had enough of a music scene to keep him satisfied for a while, but deep down, Joy always knew this moment was coming. If the holiday tour went well, The Hero's Journey would probably offer Danny full membership in the band, and then the chances of him returning to Emerald Hill would be pretty slim.

She felt like she was saying goodbye to him forever.

"I better get in there," he said, pulling a hastily-packed duffel bag and his guitar case out of the trunk of Joy's car. "They'll kill me if I miss my flight."

"Yeah, that wouldn't be a good first impression," Joy agreed, her voice a little shaky. She'd promised herself she wouldn't be emotional in this moment, and in fact she'd been subconsciously steeling herself for it for quite some time, but it was hard not to think about how much she'd miss her best friend while he was touring the south central United States and living his dream.

"Hey," he said, picking up on her emotion. "I'll be back in a few weeks."

"Sure you will," she said with a wry smile. She knew that The Hero's Journey was based in Tennessee, and if he became a member he'd have to move there, too.

For now, Danny shrugged and said, "Hey, all my crap's still in the apartment so you *know* I have to come back for it."

"Yeah, you wouldn't want to be separated from your framed *Die Hard* poster for too long," Joy said with a snort. She'd teased him relentlessly about his choice of décor ever since they moved in together after high school, and in the intervening five years she started to think that he kept that particular relic of his teen years hanging over the living room couch just to spite her.

"That is an American classic," Danny answered firmly, but he couldn't keep a straight face. He pulled Joy in for one last hug, his guitar case thumping against her shin, and then he pulled away and said, "Hey, I want the Emerald Hill gossip. Keep me posted on your resort guests' crazy antics."

"Of course," Joy promised.

She'd been working at the Emerald Mountain Ski Resort ever since high school and Christmas time on the picturesque, snowy mountainside was always the busiest time of year. With a fully booked resort always came a few crazies, and Joy would come home from work at night and regale Danny with stories of the strange and extravagant requests they came up with. It wouldn't be the same this year without him, but she'd find a way to get through it.

"And find yourself a girlfriend," he said with a wink. "You work too hard."

"Yeah, right," Joy said with a roll of her eyes. She'd had a couple of short flings with resort guests over the years, but Danny himself knew how hard it was to find something permanent in a town built around seasonal tourism.

Then Danny turned and walked into the airport, and Joy climbed quickly back into her car. She didn't want to linger on the sidewalk where her tears would begin to threaten again, and it was too cold to stand outside for long anyway. She could see her breath as she turned her keys in the ignition, rubbing her hands together and trying to get warm again. There were only ten days til Christmas, and that was good news – it meant that Joy would have plenty of work to do at the resort to keep her mind off the very real possibility of losing her best friend.

Her manager had told her at the beginning of the winter season that he saw management potential in her, and that he would have time to mentor her after the holiday rush died down. Of course, Danny's response when she told him had been to snort and say, "Who wants that? We both need to get out of Emerald Hill and start living our lives."

He was probably right, and if Joy needed any further

kick in the pants to start looking for jobs in places that had a more permanent air then his departure provided that motivation. But change was hard, and she had the holiday rush to get through first.

TWO

CARMEN

Carmen Castillo was sitting in one corner of a big, velvet-lined booth at The Palms in Manhattan. Her family was flying out to the Emerald Mountain Ski Resort first thing in the morning for a ski holiday that her father had booked, and Carmen was squeezing in a few more hours with her friends before the trip.

"Why *Colorado?*" her best friend, Brigid, was asking her, shouting over the music in the club. "What's wrong with Cancun?"

"Nothing," she said with a sigh.

The Castillos had gone to Cancun every year for the last ten Christmases, ever since her dad's 'silly inventions' turned into the not-so-silly source of their vacation funds. That was where Brigid and her family were headed this Christmas, and when Carmen's dad announced his intention to fly the family to Emerald Hill this year, she realized that she had gotten used to seeing palm trees and sand on Christmas morning. It was a nice respite from the bitter cold of New York winters, and she was missing her lounge chair by the pool already.

"He wants the twins to experience a white Christmas," she explained. Her sisters, born almost exactly nine months after her dad's big break, had never seen snow on Christmas day, and Carmen had to admit that there was something a bit more festive about a world blanketed in sparkling, pure white snow than an artificial Christmas tree with a view of the beach. She added with a smirk, "I think he's gone nostalgic on us."

She wondered if nostalgia was really the right word, though.

The last time she'd seen snow at Christmas, Carmen had been thirteen years old and her parents had been on the verge of losing the tiny house the three of them cohabited in Massachusetts. Her mother was working ten-hour days as a nurse's aide and her father had been laid off from his factory job, so he spent his days coming up with invention after invention in the vain hope that one of them would pay off and save the family. They hadn't had much for Christmas that year, and it wasn't a memory that any of them had romanticized.

Maybe sentimental was a better word. They were about to spend ten days in a luxury cabin in the mountains, and the twins would end up with a much more idyllic memory of their first Christmas in the snow than Carmen ever had. She wondered if her father was chasing traditional Christmas cheer this year as a way of replacing those impoverished memories with better ones.

"I just can't imagine *choosing* snow," Brigid said,

shaking her head sympathetically at Carmen. "If it were up to me, I'd live on the beach year-round."

"Me too," shouted a guy's voice, and then Brigid's boyfriend, Bentley, slumped into the booth beside her. Carmen rolled her eyes – she wasn't a fan of Bentley or the influence he'd been having on her best friend lately – and he made a show of kissing Brigid. When their lips finally parted, he said, "Hey babe, whatcha up to?"

"It's Carmen's last night in New York," she said. "I'm just wishing her well on her ski trip into the icy tundra of Colorado."

"It's not going to be that bad," Carmen said with a laugh. "It's actually warmer in Denver than in New York."

"You don't strike me as the outdoors type," Bentley said, appraising Carmen.

Brigid had picked him up like a virus at the State University of New York and Carmen knew it had been a bad idea to go their separate ways for college. Now they were almost six months post-graduation and she still hadn't been able to shake him. Bentley was the epitome of a New York trust fund kid, as were most of the people that Carmen spent her days with in her private high school and then at Cornell. Brigid was the exception and it was why Carmen liked her so much, but the longer she dated Bentley, the more he corrupted Brigid and the more Carmen disliked him.

When she didn't respond right away, preferring to pretend that the music was too loud rather than engaging with him, Bentley added, jabbing Brigid with his elbow,

"She's probably going to turn into Jack Nicholson in *The Shining* up in those mountains. 'All work and no play makes Carmen a dull girl.'"

"Yeah, well, at least some of us know how to work," Carmen said, mumbling the insult under her breath. It would have been so much more satisfying to say it loud enough for Bentley to hear, but as much as she wished Brigid would see his spoiled rich kid attitude for what it was, she couldn't bring herself to be outright cruel – ahem, honest – to her best friend's boyfriend right in front of her. Out loud she said, "I'm going to get another drink. Anyone need a refill?"

"No," Brigid said, pointing to the half-filled vodka cranberry sitting on the table in front of her. Then Bentley wrapped his arms around her and they resumed their exaggerated public display of affection, his tongue snaking into her mouth before Carmen turned away.

The club was crowded as usual and it took her a while to get over to the bar. She didn't even care about getting a drink – she just needed to get out of that booth for a minute. Carmen hadn't noticed the change coming over her best friend right away. It had been subtle, but the longer Bentley stuck around, the more Brigid had begun to match his shallow, materialistic and self-centered personality. Worst of all, it was rare to get through an evening without him popping up wherever they were. Even though Carmen had tried to broach the subject delicately with Brigid a few times ("I don't know if you've noticed, but you're dating an asshole," hadn't seemed quite right, but, "Do you *really* like that Bentley guy?"

hadn't gotten the message across either) it never seemed to help and she felt increasingly sure that she was losing her best friend to the vapid rich kid crowd.

While Carmen was waiting for her turn to catch the bartender's attention, a guy with slicked-back hair and a designer suit jacket slid up to the bar beside her.

"Hey," he shouted to her over the music. "Busy night."

"Yeah," she answered distractedly, trying to keep her eye on the bartender, otherwise she knew she'd be standing here all night.

The guy leaned over the bar the next time the bartender walked past and managed to flag him down. Then he turned to Carmen and said with a toothy grin, "What are you drinking, sweetheart?"

"Oh," she said, feeling her cheeks beginning to burn. "It's okay, I'll get my own drink."

"No strings attached," he said, still smiling at her. She knew this wasn't exactly true – no man has ever bought a girl a drink without any expectations – but he seemed good-natured, and she knew the chances of flagging the bartender down again were slim, so she gave him her drink order.

"Thanks," she said, and then because they had to kill the time until the bartender came back with their orders, she said, "How's your night going?"

"Better now that you're here," he answered in the typically cliché fashion of most of the men she met in clubs like this. His eyes made a quick sweep over her – unfortunately not quick enough to avoid detection, and she couldn't wait to get her drink and make her way back to Brigid.

Carmen tried to dress as conservatively as she could in places like this to avoid interactions like the one she was currently having. Tonight she was wearing a black dress with long sleeves and a high neckline, the most clothing one could get away with wearing to a club in Manhattan, even if it was December. Meanwhile Brigid's wardrobe had grown increasingly skimpy ever since the advent of Bentley, as if she had to continually convince him that he was still interested in her – another strike against him in Carmen's mind.

"I appreciate that," Carmen said. "But you're not my type."

She'd become somewhat of an expert at deflecting unwanted advances ever since Brigid had endeavored to immerse herself in the club scene – Carmen, on the other hand, would take a good coffee shop over this place any day.

"Tall, dark and handsome?" he asked, still grinning at her.

Thankfully the bartender returned at long last with her martini and his scotch on the rocks. Carmen pulled a twenty-dollar bill out of the slim purse slung over her shoulder and threw it on the bar. It was the smallest bill she had, but she found it well worth leaving a generous tip to extract herself from this uncomfortable moment.

"Male," Carmen answered, and then slipped into the crowd without waiting for his reaction. If she knew anything about the guys who hung around clubs trying to pick up women, he would simply stay by the bar until another girl needed a drink and play the whole scene over again until one of them thought that he really was tall, dark and handsome.

When she got back to the booth, Brigid and Bentley were still completely absorbed in each other and it looked like Carmen had lost the attention of her best friend for the night. She could have sat back down and watched herself become the third wheel, or she could have tried to mingle on the dance floor, but this wasn't her scene and she had an early flight to catch. So instead, she set one of the most expensive martinis she'd ever ordered down on the table and shouted over the music, "Hey, I got you a martini. I think I'm going to head home."

"Already?" Brigid asked, genuine alarm in her voice. She popped up from the booth and pulled Carmen aside, talking to her confidentially. "It's not because Bentley's here, is it?"

Carmen didn't have the heart to tell her that it *definitely* had to do with Bentley's presence – not mere hours before they would be separated for almost two weeks. So she shook her head and said, "No, I'm just tired, and I still need to pack a few things for the plane."

"Oh, okay," Brigid said. "Well, call me when you get into Denver, and take lots of pictures."

"Try not to freeze solid," Bentley shouted from where he was spread out in the booth.

"Yeah, thanks for your concern," Carmen said.

"We'll send you pictures from Cancun," he said, "so you don't feel too left out."

Carmen resisted the urge to roll her eyes as she asked Brigid, low enough that Bentley couldn't hear, "He's coming with you?"

"Yeah," Brigid said. "He's never been at Christmas time."

It felt like the final domino in a line, all falling toward the conclusion that she was losing her best friend to this idiot who was apparently so charming that she couldn't see how self-absorbed he was. There was nothing Carmen could do at nearly midnight the night before she was leaving the state, though, so she just smiled weakly and said, "I hope you have a great trip, and a Merry Christmas."

"You too, honey," Brigid said, pulling Carmen into a hug. "We're exchanging gifts after we get back, right?"

"Yeah," Carmen said. "I'm looking forward to it."

"Me too," Brigid said with a broad smile, but then Bentley snagged her arm and pulled her back into the booth. She landed with a giggle on his lap and before Carmen was subjected to whatever was going to follow that, she turned and wove her way out of the club.

DECEMBER 17

THREE
CARMEN

The plane ride was a quick four and a half hours into Denver. Carmen had stayed up late the night before packing all of the new clothes she'd bought for the trip, carefully removing tags and folding them into her suitcases, so she fell asleep shortly after take-off. She slipped her favorite lavender sleep mask over her eyes and put in a pair of ear plugs to drown out the noise of the other passengers – particularly her kid sisters, who spent most of the trip watching movies on an iPad that they propped on the tray table directly behind Carmen's seat.

The next time she opened her eyes, it was because Carmen felt someone nudging her arm. She lifted her sleep mask and saw her dad pointing at the window beside her, and when she took out her ear plugs, he said, "Check it out. We're flying over the mountain."

She leaned over to look out the window and he stood

looking over her shoulder, trying to get the twins to pause their movie for a moment to enjoy the view.

"Marisol, Maria, look before you miss it," he said, and Carmen's mom gave a little laugh from her seat. The twins clearly took after her because she was just as absorbed in her own tablet.

"They're mountains, honey," she said. "I think they'll be there for a while."

"Wow," Carmen said as she took in the view. The sky was clear with no clouds to obscure their view and the earth below them was a long stretch of perfectly untouched, snow-capped mountains. She laughed and said, "It looks like someone dumped a big box of baking soda on the earth."

"A few *tons* of baking soda," Marisol said behind her. Dad must have convinced them to look up from their movie after all.

"We're going to have so much fun this week," he said, sitting back down in his seat across the aisle from Carmen after they had passed the majority of the snow caps. "We've got less than half an hour before we reach the airport. You guys want to go over the itinerary now?"

He dug a packet out of his carry-on bag and it was at least twenty pages thick. Carmen's dad was nothing if not thorough, and he'd only lightened up on the itineraries last year because they'd been to Cancun so many times that there was nothing left to plan that they hadn't already done. Carmen suspected it was a large part of why he'd decided they were going to change their destination this year – a vacation wasn't fun for Dad unless he got to plan it.

"You and your itineraries," their mom said. "Honey, everybody just wants to go shopping and hang out at the lodge."

The twins' eyes lit up at the mention of shopping, and Dad said, "Don't worry, dear, shopping is *definitely* on the itinerary. I know my girls like to shop."

"What else do you have planned, Dad?" Carmen asked, taking pity on him.

The twins and Mom had a way of ganging up on him sometimes – the three of them had embraced the luxury lifestyle more than Carmen and Dad, and a lot of the time she felt like it was her responsibility to stand by him as one of the members of the family who remembered what it was like before his lucky break. She couldn't blame Marisol and Maria for their tendency toward materialism – they were born into money in a way that Carmen could never understand – but sometimes she did wish her mother had a better memory of the little rundown house they'd started from.

"Tonight once we get settled in, we've got reservations at the Indigo Steakhouse," he said. "They've got the best Kobe beef in Colorado, and their dessert menu is supposed to be out of this world. I know you girls are going to enjoy that."

"What do they have?" Maria asked, perking up and leaning over Marisol. Dad handed her a menu that he'd printed out.

"Anything you can imagine, baby girl," he said, then

went back to his packet while the twins drooled over the dessert menu together. "Tomorrow we'll go into town and get some shopping done – I know that's all you care about, Lucia."

"That's right," Mom said with a small laugh. "I appreciate you remembering my priorities, honey."

"I also booked a sled dog excursion that sounds like a lot of fun, and the resort has some festivities planned that we can check out," he continued. He had another half-page of activities listed, with corresponding brochures, menus, and reservation details which would keep them all occupied until it was time to fasten their seatbelts and prepare for the descent into Denver International Airport.

Carmen popped a stick of gum into her mouth to keep her ears from popping, passing the pack around to the rest of her family and then chewing away. She didn't mind flying – she'd been on at least a half-dozen planes every year for the last decade – but the descent was something she would skip if she could.

❄

THE AIRPORT WAS CROWDED with people and filled with an excited energy. Most of them were either flying in for a mountain vacation like the Castillos, or flying out to visit family, and everyone was quite a bit more cheerful than Carmen usually found travelers at airports to be.

The main terminal of the airport was wide, with

uniquely peaked ceilings that Carmen's dad was enamored with the moment they stepped out of the concourse. As they made their way to the transportation counter to call the limousine Dad had arranged for, they passed a half-dozen Christmas trees lined up in the center of the terminal, the smell of cinnamon and pine mixing to give Carmen a sudden case of the same sentimentality that must have beckoned her dad to Emerald Hill.

"Look, the mountains aren't far away," she said to her sisters, putting her hands on their shoulders and physically turning them to face the large windows that pointed toward the mountains. Marisol and Maria reluctantly slipped their phones into their pockets and looked at the mountain range rising up in the distance, snow streaked across it.

"It *is* pretty," Mom admitted. "Nothing like that first blast of warm air when you step outside in Cancun, though. I'm shivering just looking out there."

"You're exaggerating, dear," Dad said as he rejoined the group. "Besides, I seem to remember that a certain someone usually only makes it a few hours down there before she starts griping about the heat."

"Maybe so," Mom admitted.

"The limo is going to meet us at the pick-up spot out front," he said. "We should head over there."

It took a little while to get all of their luggage loaded into the trunk, and a few of their suitcases had to ride in the back with the family. Mom and the twins always liked to bring extra luggage whenever they went on vacation because it was easier than arranging to have the things that they purchased on vacation shipped back to New York. For them, most of the fun was in shopping at stores that they didn't have in the city and bringing back unique wardrobe pieces and décor items for the house.

Carmen had brought her fair share of luggage, too. She didn't care as much about vacation shopping as her mom and sisters, but she did like to have an overabundance of wardrobe choices and that always necessitated a minimum of two large bags. Dad was the only one among them who could be classified as a light packer, and he stood around mildly bored and irritated after his single suitcase was neatly loaded into the trunk and he still had to wait for six or seven more bags to be fitted into the limo like a Tetris game.

Finally, the Castillos and all their luggage piled into the limousine and they were headed out of Denver. It was about an hour's drive from the airport to the small town of Emerald Hill where the resort was located, and the twins had gone right back to their iPad to finish up the movie they'd been watching on the plane. Mom immersed herself in the book she'd been reading – some murder mystery that she'd picked up at LaGuardia on a whim – and Carmen and her dad both watched the scenery change outside the window.

The land immediately around the airport was flat, optimal for landing planes, but after a while the prairie-like scenery gave way to pine trees dotting the side of the road, growing larger and more forested.

"That's Emerald Mountain, straight ahead," Dad said as the earth rose up directly in front of them, growing larger and more breath-taking the closer they got. When they got to a part of the road that began to incline and follow the curve of the mountain, Carmen leaned her forehead against the window, feeling the cold glass against her skin as she craned her head to see the mountains rising up all around her.

"That's really something, isn't it, kiddo?" her dad asked, and he looked at his wife and younger daughters with a slightly frustrated sigh.

They were completely unimpressed with this view, and Carmen didn't see how that was possible. She'd been to the mountains before, and one summer when she was still in high school she'd convinced Brigid to hike a part of the Appalachian Trail for a day, but she'd never seen anything like this before. From the ground, the snow-covered mountains no longer reminded Carmen of baking soda. They were steep and dotted with pine trees, and they made her feel small in a very humbling way.

After a few minutes of silence from inside the limo, Carmen and Dad watching the scenery, Mom and the twins absorbed in their own worlds, Carmen took her carry-on bag out of the pile of luggage and dug out her phone. She wanted to capture the beauty of the mountains so that she could show Brigid – and Bentley too, she thought grudgingly – the benefits of a snowy Christmas vacation. Besides, she thought as she put down her window and shivered at the cold air, they would be sending her shot after shot of sunny beaches and Mexican cuisine. She wanted to have something impressive to send back.

The cold air coming through the open window roused the rest of her family, and Dad watched with satisfaction as Mom and the twins finally had no choice but to acknowledge the beauty surrounding them. Mom pulled her coat tighter around her shoulders and snuggled into Dad's side for the sake of his body heat while Marisol and Maria rolled down their own window and attempted to master the art of the moving-vehicle selfie, using the mountain as the backsplash.

"*Now* is everyone happy we came here?" Dad asked. "I'm telling you, we're going to have a great time. Nothing beats snow at Christmas."

"Maybe a margarita at a swim-up bar," Mom said, giving him a wink.

Everyone closed their windows and Carmen shivered for a minute or two, waiting for the limo to warm back up again. The mountains outside were getting taller, looming so high over the top of the car that Carmen couldn't see all of their peaks anymore. The snow was getting denser, covering the ground and the pine trees that dotted the side of the road. They must be getting close to the resort.

FOUR

JOY

It was only early afternoon and to Joy, it already felt like one of the longest days she'd ever weathered. The resort was fully booked with holiday guests – all three hundred rooms of the hotel and the twenty luxury cabins lined up in a row at the base of the ski slopes – and they were all doing their best to keep her busy.

Up until last year she'd been nothing more than a front desk clerk, and then the front desk supervisor when the job opened up and she was surprised to find that she had the most seniority of all the clerks. This year, though, her boss had a crazy idea that she was capable of taking on more responsibility and he made her a shift supervisor, which she quickly realized meant that she should invest in a good pair of shoes. For the last six months, her days consisted of running all over the resort, putting out fires and managing problems for both guests and employees. She enjoyed it, but the closer the holiday season came, the more frantic her days were.

On this day in particular, she thought it was probably a blessing to be this busy. She hadn't heard from Danny since she dropped him off at the airport, and even though she knew he was probably getting ready for the band's next tour stop, she'd hoped that he would have found a few minutes to call and fill her in on the Hero's Journey gossip. Even a text would have been nice, to know he got into Memphis okay.

Joy would call him just as soon as her shift was over, but in the meantime she found herself temporarily stuck in the lobby. They'd had a call-off for the afternoon shift, and Joy would have to return to her old front desk role until she could find someone to cover it.

That was okay, too, because there was little she loved more than watching people's eyes light up the first time they set foot inside the resort. There were a lot of people who liked it here so much that they came every year, but their expressions were nothing compared to the brand new visitors, who Joy could spot at a glance. They always looked like they had just found themselves in a strange land, their eyes wide at the majesty of the mountains. Most of them had never spent a Christmas in the mountains before, and Joy always liked making it extra special for them because she was used to this setting and the holiday rush gave her an opportunity to experience the season through fresh eyes.

She didn't have to wait long for one of these moments. Joy had only been standing behind the desk for about fifteen minutes when a family of five came into the lobby. There were two young girls, maybe around ten years old if Joy's calculations were correct, and they were both glued to their phones as they walked until their father plucked the devices out of their hands.

"Look," he said, pointing at the enormous Christmas fir that was the centerpiece of the lobby. "When's the last time you've seen a tree that big?"

Joy smiled, watching their eyes go wide as they took in the enormity of the tree sparkling with white lights and glittery ornaments. After a minute she called, her voice echoing slightly in the large lobby, "It's eighteen feet tall. I know because I was the brave soul who put the star on top."

"It's lovely," the matriarch of the family said, approaching the desk, and following lazily behind her was a girl who looked to be in her early twenties – the family's eldest daughter, perhaps. She had long, nearly-black hair with soft curls, eyes of a matching dark brown, and plump lips that she swiped her tongue over as she followed her mother to the front desk. She was beautiful, and Joy had to look quickly away before the girl noticed her gaze.

"Welcome to the Emerald Mountain Ski Resort," Joy said in her most professional tone. "Are you checking in?"

"Yes," the older woman said. She was pretty in her own right, her hair meticulously straightened and beginning to go gray, but there was no doubt where the younger woman had inherited her beauty. "The reservation is under Antonio Castillo."

Joy pulled up their information in the computer and wasn't the slightest bit surprised to find that they had reserved one of the luxury cabins for a ten-day stay. They went for about a thousand dollars a night, and Joy could tell by the meticulous manicure, the designer clothes, and the perfectly groomed look of the matriarch that the expense would be inconsequential to them. It had been one of the hardest things to get used to when she started working at the resort – the disparity between her own standard of living and that of a lot of their guests. She'd allowed herself to be intimidated by people like the Castillos in the past, and while she'd gotten over that particular hang-up, she did find it difficult to meet the eyes of the eldest daughter.

That was more about beauty than wealth, though. Joy had always had a weakness for smoldering, dark eyes.

"Umm," she said, "your cabin is ready. I'll accompany you to give you the tour and make sure you have everything you need."

She passed a few key cards to Mrs. Castillo and then made a couple of quick calls – to get a bellhop to help the family with their luggage, and then to get one of the concierges to come over and watch the desk for a few minutes. Then she followed the family outside, where a black limousine was waiting with the engine running.

"You're in cabin number four," Joy told them. "I'll lead and your driver can follow me."

She and the bellhop – his name was Aaron, and he was new this year – got into one of the resort transportation vans parked not far away and she led the way down a slightly icy road into a valley. The resort, the luxury cabins, and the ski lodge were all nestled in a dip between two mountain ranges, the snow-covered slopes running down the sides of the mountains on three sides of the resort. Joy made a mental note to order the salt trucks to make another pass on this road before fresh snow came down tonight. Then they pulled up in front of cabin number four and she hopped out. The limousine pulled in behind them and Joy walked the Castillos into their accommodation while Aaron handled the luggage.

They went up the short pathway to the door, which had been meticulously shoveled and salted that morning, and every morning. Joy stepped aside for the Castillos to enter, adopting the tour guide persona that she'd gotten so good at in the last five years. "Here we are. Your home away from home."

The cabin, identical to the other nineteen all lined up in a row, was the size of a small house – and at least three times the size of Joy and Danny's apartment – and she always enjoyed this particular tour. The view was breathtaking, large windows in almost every room offering a nearly three hundred and sixty-degree view of the mountains on every side of them. Joy still hadn't quite gotten used to this view, even after five years of seeing it almost daily.

Joy watched their reactions, and every one of the Castillos paused. Even Mrs. Castillo, who seemed preoccupied with making sure that Aaron handled her luggage gently, stopped to slip her arm through her husband's to look at the view from the large picture windows in the living room. The young woman's mouth dropped open as she stepped into the cabin, and the younger girls demanded their phones back from their dad so they could document their luxurious surroundings.

"Beautiful, isn't it?" Joy asked them, and Mr. Castillo let out a loud breath.

"That's an understatement."

While Aaron brought load after load of suitcases into the entryway, Joy walked the Castillos through the space, pointing out all of the luxury features from the gas fireplace to the chef's kitchen and the Jacuzzi bathtub. There was a large Christmas tree in front of the picture windows– not quite as large as the one in the resort lobby but still plenty impressive – and the mantle was decorated with pine boughs and five stockings, one for each of the family members.

"Wow," Mr. Castillo said as he noticed this. "You people think of everything."

"We try," Joy said with a smile, and then she winked at the younger girls. "I even think Santa came a little early and left a pre-Christmas treat in those stockings."

One of them rolled her eyes at Joy and said, "I don't believe in Santa," but then she went over to the mantle and put her hands on the toe of one of the stockings, feeling for its contents.

"So is this your first trip to Emerald Mountain?" Joy asked, although she was pretty certain she already knew the answer.

She watched the young woman walking through the cabin, going to the kitchen island where a tray full of Christmas goodies had been set out – sugar cookies and hot cocoa mix and candy canes. She picked up one of the latter and peeled back the plastic wrapper, and Joy had to look away before the girl put it in her mouth for fear that she'd blush.

"Yes," Mrs. Castillo said. "We usually go someplace warm for the holidays."

"Well, you've got this warm fire to come back to when it gets too chilly," Joy said, "and all the hot cocoa, coffee, and tea you could ask for in the ski lodge."

"Sounds wonderful," Mr. Castillo said. "We're looking forward to an authentic, snowy Christmas experience."

"Great," Joy said, noticing that Aaron was standing in the doorway – a good indication that he'd finally finished with their bags, which were now stacked neatly in the entryway. "Well, I'll leave you to get settled in. If you need anything for the cabin, or if you're looking for recommendations about things to do during your visit, don't hesitate to call down to the front desk. My name is Joy if you need anything."

She made accidental eye contact with the young woman in the kitchen as she said this last part, and the candy cane in her mouth was every bit as tantalizing as Joy had expected it would be. For her part, the girl didn't seem aware of the effect she was having, and Joy couldn't figure out why she was so drawn to her. She patted Aaron on the shoulder and said, "Come on, I have to get back to the lobby."

DECEMBER 18

FIVE
JOY

Joy woke up with a start to the unfamiliar sound of her alarm clock. She hadn't needed to set it in ages, and she didn't like beginning the day with a jolt as her phone vibrated against the wood of her night table. She was used to hearing Danny playing his acoustic guitar, or plucking at the strings of his electric with the amp off. He got up early every morning and played for a few hours before his restaurant shifts, and that was always her cue to get up and begin her day.

That kind of dedication had landed him this gig with The Hero's Journey. She just wished he'd call her back so she wouldn't have to keep scanning the news for Tennessee plane crashes. She'd sent Danny a half-dozen increasingly irritated texts yesterday asking him to tell her that he got to Memphis safely and everything was going well with the band.

She had the morning free before an evening shift at the resort and there was no good reason to set her alarm, but she didn't want to sleep her way through her leisure time, which was precious around the holidays. Besides, five years of waking up early to the musical stylings of Danny had conditioned Joy to get up early – she rarely managed to sleep in, even on her days off.

So she got up and put on a heavy fleece robe to keep away the chill of the drafty apartment. It was an old building – most everything in Emerald Hill that wasn't associated with the resort was old – but Joy had gotten used to the routine of being cold. She went into the kitchen and made herself a cup of her favorite peppermint tea, stirring a candy cane into it to sweeten it up.

Her mind went to the girl she met yesterday – well, *met* was a strong word for it, but she *had* managed to make an impression on Joy. She probably wouldn't look at a candy cane again the same way for the rest of the holiday season, anyway.

Joy went into the living room as she sipped her tea, flipping a light switch on the wall to turn on the multicolored lights of the Christmas tree she and Danny had purchased the day after Thanksgiving. He'd teased her at the time, telling her it was too soon (an argument they had every year), but she'd made him put it up anyway.

"The needles are going to fall off well before Christmas," he'd objected. "You're supposed to wait until the middle of the month if you want a live tree."

"You said that last year," Joy had answered as she passed him a string of lights and he started winding them around the branches. "It was still plenty green on Christmas Day, and this way we get to enjoy it longer."

It turned out to be lucky that she hadn't let Danny sway her, because if they'd waited until he wanted to go get a tree, he would have ended up in Memphis and she'd have been stuck in an empty apartment with no Christmas cheer whatsoever. At least the tree, with its twinkling lights and festive pine aroma, brought her a little bit of comfort as she sat down in an overstuffed chair near it to finish her tea. She pulled her phone out of the pocket of her robe where she'd stashed it and checked for a message from Danny, but there was nothing.

Maybe he'd gotten swept up in getting acquainted with the band and their songs, and there was no doubt he would have a million things to do to get ready for the tour, but Joy couldn't stand not knowing what was going on with him. Danny was her oldest friend – they'd met in kindergarten and been inseparable ever since, and Joy was pretty sure that his parents *still* didn't totally believe that nothing romantic would ever come out of their relationship.

She liked to tease him about this sometimes, as if he was the one who had something to come out of the closet about, so when she called him and he didn't answer, she left him a pestering voicemail. "Hey, it's me. I'm going to tell your mom the true and shockingly platonic nature of our relationship if you don't call me back. The suspense is killing me, dude."

It was only about eight in the morning in Emerald Hill, which would make it nine in Memphis, and Joy figured there was no way even the tamest of rock musicians were already hard at work at that hour. That meant

Danny had no excuse but to find a minute to call her back. Joy finished her tea and decided that she'd spend the rest of her day on the slopes, sneaking in a few hours of snowboarding before the late shift started. She certainly didn't want to spend that time sitting around her empty apartment, looking at Danny's stupid action movie posters and feeling sorry for herself because her last Emerald Hill friend was moving on.

She cleaned her mug and put it on the counter to dry, then went back into her bedroom to get changed. She put on a pair of thick snow pants – one of the most expensive pieces of clothing she owned, and well-worth the price tag for all the use she got out of them. Free access to the slopes was Joy's favorite perk of working at the resort, and one of the reasons why she had never before considered a change of scenery. She loved the sense of peace that being alone on the mountain gave her.

She put on a thin but warm undershirt, then a lightweight ski jacket that would keep her warm and dry no matter what the slope conditions were. She packed her work uniform into a duffel bag that she could keep in her car and change into before her shift, then she went into the living room and pulled a pair of boots out of the closet by the front door. She stepped into them, then retrieved her pride and joy from the back of the closet – the snowboard her mother had bought for her the day she graduated from high school.

They had gone together to the sporting goods store right after the ceremony, and her mom had shaken her head at Joy as she watched her examine every single board in the shop. "You know you can't use that until next year. Don't you want something a little more practical for your graduation gift?"

"This'll be plenty practical in a couple of months," Joy had objected as she pulled a beautiful board with a woodgrain finish off the rack.

"Careful, honey, I think you're drooling," her mother had said with a laugh. "Is that the one?"

"Yeah," she said, running her hand along the smooth finish of the board. She'd boarded every single winter since then with it, and spent quite a lot of her free time with this board. It was just the thing to keep her mind off what was going on in Memphis until Danny finally found the time to call her back.

SIX

CARMEN

Carmen and her family went down into the small town of Emerald Hill after they got settled into the cabin. It was about a fifteen-minute drive from the resort, and it seemed like most of the town's businesses, restaurants, and shops were situated along one long stretch down the main road. They ate at the Indigo Restaurant, the twins taking about an hour to decide between the many items on the dessert menu, and in the end Dad told the waiter to bring a half-dozen things to the table along with five forks.

Carmen was savoring a salted caramel-topped molten lava cake, the dark chocolate oozing across the plate as she tried in vain to fend off her sisters' forks, when her dad pulled out the itinerary packet again to groans around the table.

"Can't we just play it by ear, honey?" Mom asked. "You're the only one who enjoys highly structured vacations."

"Ah," Dad objected, holding up a finger to motion for silence. "Tomorrow is shopping day. Do any of you really intend to complain about that? An entire day in Denver, where you can shop your hearts out and I will wait patiently and carry the bags and *not* complain, because I've got Christmas spirit."

"We've got Christmas spirit, yes we do," Maria said, turning Dad's words into a cheer. Marisol chimed in for the second half, and they said in unison, "We've got Christmas spirit, how about you?"

Then the little snake, Maria, took a stab at the molten lava cake that Carmen had been trying to keep for herself.

"Hey," she objected, but in the end, she pushed the plate toward the center of the table and reached for a chocolate chip cookie with melting vanilla ice cream on top instead.

❄

THIS MORNING CARMEN woke up to her mother gently shaking her shoulder.

"Hey, honey," she was saying, "time to get up. We've got a long day of shopping ahead of us."

"What time is it?" Carmen mumbled, putting her hand over her eyes. The early morning light was reflecting off the snow outside her window and it seemed impossibly bright despite the fact that she felt like she'd hardly slept. She had gone to bed around midnight, but then Brigid started inundating Carmen's phone with pictures and videos from her arrival in Cancun, and she hadn't managed to get to sleep until after one.

"It's still early," Mom said. "But the drive into Denver is going to take about an hour, and I'm sure you'll want time to get ready and have some breakfast. The resort sent a basket of scones."

"Five more minutes," Carmen whined, wanting nothing more than to throw the blankets over her head and try to block out the light so she could sleep a little longer. She'd been working for her dad full-time ever since she graduated from college and sleeping late was a luxury she didn't have in New York.

"Okay," her mom said in a tone that implied she didn't understand her eldest daughter. Carmen knew that Marisol and Maria would never drag their feet when it came to an opportunity to spend money lavishly – it was their favorite hobby, and in that way they were their mother's children. Carmen sometimes felt like an outsider in her own family, and sometimes she wondered if her mother even remembered the tiny, worn-down little house that Carmen spent the first thirteen years of her life in.

Her mom left the room and Carmen pulled up the big, plush comforter to block out the sun, falling instantly back to sleep.

The next time she woke up, the sun was higher in the sky and the cabin was unexpectedly quiet. Carmen sat up with a jolt, the feeling of oversleeping her alarm coursing through her as she realized it had been much longer than five minutes. She grabbed her phone off the night table beside the bed and saw that it was almost ten – according to Dad's itinerary, they should have been in Denver by now.

Carmen jumped out of bed and threw on one of the resort's plush robes as she rushed into the living room, wondering if everyone was waiting for her, and if they were angry that she'd held them up. Instead, the cabin was empty and Carmen found a note on the kitchen island, leaning against the aforementioned basket of scones.

Carmen,

You were sleeping so peacefully when I came back in, I decided not to wake you. Get the rest you need and if you want to join us in Denver, call and I'll send a car. We're going to Sushi Den for lunch.

Love,
Mom

By the time she finished reading the note, Carmen went from anxious to irritated. It was true that she hadn't been particularly eager to spend the entire day buying unnecessary clothes, but she hadn't expected her family to just leave without her. Being an adult still felt new to her sometimes, and she wondered if this was another byproduct – her parents never would have left her sisters behind, but now apparently she was old enough to need rest more than a new pair of boots, and they hadn't thought much of going to Denver without her.

Even if she was supposed to be an adult who was

independent and unbothered by things like that, she felt a little hurt that they would have left without her. She went back to her room and pulled a pair of jeans out of her luggage, followed by a large, chunky knit sweater, and got dressed. She pulled her hair into a quick ponytail, then went back into the kitchen, reading her mom's note again. She could spend an hour in the car to eat sushi in Denver, but she was feeling a little salty about the whole thing and she decided that she'd just fend for herself.

She grabbed one of the scones – a cranberry one with orange glaze on top that practically melted in her mouth – and sat down at the island, texting her mom to let her know she was going to stay at the resort today.

Then while she ate, Carmen habitually opened and scrolled through each of the social media feeds on her phone. They were all flooded with pictures of the beach, the ocean, and an equal number of couple selfies from Brigid and Bentley.

Carmen rolled her eyes at the stupid faces he was pulling, but under one of the pictures she typed, "So cute. Hope you're having fun, Brig!"

Before she'd even polished off her scone, Brigid was messaging her back.

Thanks, it's seventy-eight and sunny – wish you were here!

Carmen laughed, thinking that at this particular moment she kind of wished she was in Cancun, too, even if Bentley *was* there. She and Brigid messaged back and forth for a few minutes, and Carmen couldn't quite bring herself to tell Brigid that the mountains were beautiful and the food was good but that she was feeling lonely right now. They hadn't had that kind of close relationship since college, so she settled for sending Brigid the picture she'd taken yesterday during the ride into the mountains.

Are you a snow bunny yet? Dominate any black diamonds lately?

Brigid's reply made Carmen laugh, until the next message came through.

Ugh, sorry, Bentley grabbed my phone. He's so goofy.

Then before Carmen realized what she was doing, she started typing a response. She wasn't going to let Bentley poke fun at her from all the way across the Gulf of Mexico, so she wrote back, "Actually, I'm about to go for my first run of the day. I'll snap a picture for you from the top of the slopes."

Then she smacked herself in the forehead. It was too late because the message had already been sent, but that definitely had not been on her to-do list today. Brigid sent back a final message, and Carmen just laughed.

Oh wow, you're really embracing the winter vibes, huh? Well, I can't wait to see that!

She sighed and put down her phone, polishing off the

last crumbs of her scone and washing it down with a small bottle of orange juice that she found in the refrigerator. At least now she knew what she'd be doing today, thanks to her big mouth.

❄

CARMEN CALLED a resort transport van to take her over to the lodge, asking to be dropped off at the ski rental area. It was packed and a little overwhelming, dozens of people making their way through the line and loading up with rental skis and snowboards in order to hit the slopes. She couldn't help feeling a little bit grumpy at the sight of all the families here – meanwhile her own family was in Denver.

She was a big girl, though, and she reminded herself as the line inched slowly forward that she didn't like marathon-length shopping trips, anyway. Carmen looked out the windows while she waited in line, and from the ski rental area on the ground floor of the lodge, the mountain seemed like nothing more than a snowy hill. The windows down here weren't tall enough to showcase the full majesty of the mountain, and all Carmen could see was the bunny slopes with a few dozen novice skiers making their wobbly way down the hills.

It reminded her of the gentle slopes not far away from her childhood home. They were nothing special, but a Massachusetts winter would see quite a bit of snowfall and the hills were steep enough to build up good speed on a sled. She and Dad went sledding a lot when she was younger, and even though Mom was never the outdoorsy type, she'd always have hot cocoa or tea waiting for them when they came back into the house with their cheeks rosy and their fingers a little on the numb side.

There were no sled riders on the hill outside the ski rental area, though. Even the youngest kids were on skis or shorter versions that Carmen heard a family in front of her refer to as snowblades. And they were all doing a much better job of staying on their feet than Carmen imagined she'd be doing when she got out there.

When it was her turn at the rental counter, a rental area attendant fitted her for a pair of large, heavy boots that turned out to be pretty difficult to walk in. They were made of hard plastic and kept her ankles slightly bent at all times, and it was fortunate for Carmen that the attendant let her cling to his arm while she wobbled her way over to the rack of skis at the end of the line, clutching the snow boots she'd worn over from the cabin.

He let go of her and she put one hand on the counter just to be safe, and then he reached for a pair of scuffed, neon yellow skis that were a little wider at the tips than in the middle.

"Could I have those ones?" Carmen asked, pointing at a pair of shiny red skis at the other end of the rack.

They looked new, and furthermore they were thinner than most of the skis on the rack and looked easier to control. Carmen thought that if her big mouth was going to get her out on the slopes, then she should at least have a pretty pair of skis to accompany her in the picture she promised Bentley.

"You don't want those," the attendant said. "They're cross-country skis, and they're men's skis, anyway. They'd be much too long for you. You need a good pair of downhills."

Carmen thought fleetingly that she could go to the pro shop and buy a nice set of skis, but when would she ever use them after this week was over? She took the garishly bright neon skis that he'd selected for her, along with a set of poles, and it turned out to be quite a task to juggle skis, poles, and her boots as she wobbled away from the counter. She glanced back at the bunny slopes outside the window and thought this was going to be harder than she anticipated.

She sat down on a bench in front of a row of lockers, watching kids less than half her age dominating the bunny slopes, and wondered what on earth had possessed her to tell Brigid – and Bentley – that she was going to the top of the slopes. In these ridiculous boots, she'd be lucky to make it *outside*, and if she was being honest, she had no business being on even the most gradual of hills without a ski lesson. She didn't even know the mechanics of skiing, or simple things like how to stop.

Carmen was no great athlete, but she figured that was probably a skill she should learn if she didn't want to spend Christmas in traction.

She was here now, though, and pure stubbornness to keep her best friend's attention made Carmen determined to get the picture that she'd promised. So she hatched a plan to fake it – Brigid had never been skiing before, and she wouldn't be able to tell *how* Carmen got the shot as long as she found an impressive place on the mountainside to snap a quick selfie. She wouldn't have to go far – the entire area was a picturesque dream.

She took off the ski boots – not without a fair bit of difficulty – and put them in one of the lockers, then put her own boots back on. Then she left the skis leaning up against a wall, hoping that they'd be in an inconspicuous place until she came back and returned them with the boots. She took the poles – they'd be important to make the photo look authentic, and they'd probably also make the hike she was about to embark on easier.

Carmen went outside, shivering as the cold wind whipped across the open area at the base of the mountain. She zipped her coat, a down-insulated ski jacket that she'd bought in New York just before the trip, and then took a moment to look around.

She realized that the view of the mountain she'd gotten from the car on the way into Emerald Hill, and then from the cabin windows, had not done it any justice at all. She thought she felt small while the limousine was winding its way up into Emerald Mountain, but now Carmen felt her breath being stolen away. The hills rose up from three different directions around the resort, bigger than any skyscraper she'd encountered in New York. There were at least a dozen skiing trails she could see branching off and extending up the mountain, and where she was standing was the point at which all of it converged.

She felt tiny and significant all at once, and no photograph could ever capture that feeling. Carmen took a deep breath, and the air that stung slightly in her lungs smelled faintly of pine. The snow had its own smell, something clean and crisp she couldn't quite put her finger on, and suddenly she felt invigorated and ready for the hike up the mountainside.

SEVEN

JOY

The fresh powder on the slopes did Joy just as much good as she was hoping for. She got to the resort fairly early and by the time she made it to the top of her favorite hill, there still weren't too many people who had ventured beyond the lodge and the bunny slopes.

She took a few runs down the long and winding hill, enjoying the solitude of the mountain. It was at least a ten-minute journey to the bottom of this particular hill, not challenging like the moguls or steep like the black diamonds, and Joy never failed to feel peaceful by the time she got to the bottom. Under the wide-open sky, with few snowboarders and skiers around, it was always a good place to commune with the mountain and find a little inner stillness.

As she took her third run of the day, cutting from side to side on her snowboard, she enjoyed the wind in her hair, the cold air reddening her cheeks and nose. She took the curves of and hills with ease, turning her brain off completely – it was second nature to her by now, with no need to think about anything at all out here. She'd been memorizing every dip and curve of these hills since she was three years old, and some time with a blank mind was exactly what she needed right now.

She was just approaching a small hill, one that she always gathered speed for because she loved catching some air on it, when she saw something dark against the snow in front of her.

It caught her eye and as she approached, it got bigger. Just as Joy crested the hill, the full figure came into view – raven-black hair, then shoulders, then a girl in a white jacket. Joy pivoted in an attempt to stop, but it was too late and her snowboard lifted off at the top of the hill. All she could do was shout, "Hey!"

It wasn't much of a warning, but it was all Joy could manage.

The young woman looked up, surprise on her face, and Joy had just enough time to recognize her as the eldest daughter of the Castillo family. Then she was crashing, snowboard first, into her.

It was a violent collision. Joy dug her board into the snow as much as she could to keep from smashing it straight into the girl's legs, and then she was jerked forward, her body connecting painfully with the girl's and then tumbling head over heels down the hill. Cold snow was packed down the front of her jacket and inside her gloves when she lifted herself up from her resting place, a few feet away from the girl. Her hands hurt from trying to catch herself, and the binding had snapped off her snowboard and was still affixed to her boot.

"Shit," Joy said, then looked over at the girl, who was sitting in the snow and clutching her ankle. "You okay? Anything broken?"

"Jury's out," the girl said through clenched teeth. "Your snowboard hit my ankle and it hurts like hell."

Joy stood up, shivering and trying to shake the snow out of her coat as she went over to the girl. She crouched in the snow beside her, her heart starting to beat a little faster at the proximity. She ignored this reaction and gently pulled the girl's hands away from her ankle. "Let me see."

She pulled off her gloves, rubbing her hands together for a second to try to warm them up, and then she felt the girl's ankle, her heart inching its way up into her throat. Joy was no expert – beyond basic first aid, this was one area of resort operations in which she had no training – but nothing looked abnormally bent or swollen, and it was probably just a sprain.

"Looks like you're going to live," Joy said, hazarding a smile. The girl was even more beautiful close up, and suddenly Joy became aware of how close she'd gotten to her. She took her hands off the girl's ankle and stood up. "I think we both got lucky."

"Doesn't feel like luck," the girl said with a snort.

"Do you think you can make it down the mountain?" Joy asked.

"Yeah," the girl said. "I'll be fine."

Joy extended her hand to help her up, but as soon as

the girl put weight on her ankle she sucked air in through her clenched teeth and Joy could tell she was in more pain than she wanted to admit.

"It's sprained," Joy said. "We better get you a medic."

"No," the girl said adamantly, trying again to put some weight on her injured ankle. She limped a step or two, but it would be days before she made it back to the resort at that pace.

"Don't be silly," Joy said. "I'll call ski patrol and they'll come pick you up in a snowmobile."

"That's so embarrassing," the girl said, looking away from Joy.

"It's not a big deal," Joy said. "I work at the resort, and it happens more often than you'd think."

"I know," the girl said, and the way she looked at Joy could have melted all the snow off the hill. Those eyes were so deep, so warm, Joy had to busy herself with digging her phone out of her pocket as the girl said, "I remember you."

I remember you, too, Joy thought, a little bit of color coming to her cheeks, as she dialed the number for the medics. She went over and retrieved her snowboard, setting it on the ground behind the girl and saying, "Sit down before you hurt your ankle worse."

EIGHT

CARMEN

Carmen sat down obediently on the snowboard, although her jeans were already pretty wet. She tried not to shiver as she watched Joy complete the final step in her humiliating moment. She'd remembered the girl's name because when she said it yesterday, it had sounded like such a perfect complement to her surroundings.

As Carmen watched her call down to the lodge, she got an opportunity to really look at Joy for the first time, and she decided that the name suited her, as well as her surroundings. She had sparkling sapphire eyes and her nose was reddened by the cold in an oddly endearing way. She wore a fleece headband to protect her ears from the elements, and it flattened her chin-length blonde hair down to her cheeks. She didn't seem even the slightest bit inconvenienced by this accident, but then again, she was a resort employee – she got paid to be nice to dummies like Carmen when they hiked their way up slopes they had no business on.

"Hey, it's Joy," she said into the phone. "I'm going to need a medic on the Outer Limits slope."

She explained what happened as Carmen felt her cheeks growing more and more flushed, and at one point Joy covered the phone speaker with her hand and asked, "What's your name, hon?"

"Carmen," she said. "Castillo."

Joy repeated her name to the medic, and then after a few more details, she hung up and turned to Carmen. "I told them you're probably not dying, so they said it'll be about five minutes."

"Thanks," Carmen said. This was absolutely not how she'd imagined today going, and as she thought about the impossibility of getting that bragging photograph now, she realized that she'd lost her phone in the collision.

She started looking around, not mobile enough to get off the snowboard and really hunt for it, and Joy asked, "What are you looking for?"

"I lost my phone in the crash," Carmen explained. "It must be around here somewhere."

Joy helped her look, walking slowly around the point of collision. She walked around the area in a slow circle, widening her perimeter as she looked down at the powdery snow. It looked so light and fluffy that Carmen figured the odds of finding the phone were probably pretty slim. Joy confirmed it when she said, "It's pretty wet out here today. The phone is probably ruined."

Then she paused and furrowed her brows, looking at Carmen with a curious expression.

"What?"

"Umm, where are your skis?" Joy asked. "The poles are right there, sticking out of the snow, and my snowboard didn't go far, but I don't see your skis anywhere."

Carmen looked sheepishly down at her ankle. It was throbbing and she was feeling increasingly thankful for Joy's insistence on calling the medic. She looked back at Joy and figured she'd be losing her last shred of dignity as she said, "At the lodge."

"What?" Joy asked with a laugh. "What does that mean?"

"I hiked up here," Carmen admitted, trying to sound as confident as possible just in case she could convince Joy that hiking up the side of ski slopes was a thing that people did. It was going to be a tough sell, but she thought she might die of embarrassment if she didn't at least try.

"You did?" Joy asked.

"Do I look like I belong on a hill like this?" Carmen asked, getting a little bit frustrated at the amusement Joy seemed to be getting out of this revelation. She was the type of person who cried easily when she was frustrated, and that was the *last* thing she wanted to do right now, so she forced herself to laugh instead.

"No, you really don't," Joy said, and then she nodded at the snowboard. She said, "Scoot over, will you?"

Carmen slid over to one end of the board and Joy sat down next to her. She pulled the broken binding off her boot and tossed it in the snow a few feet away. Then she checked the time and told Carmen that the medic should be there any minute, and to Carmen's surprise, she pinched the wet fabric of her jeans on the side of her knee. The gesture felt a little familiar, or maybe it was just their proximity on the snowboard. It ignited something in Carmen, and she became a little more aware of Joy's body so near to hers as Joy said, "Blue jeans, snow boots, no skis... what on earth were you doing out here?"

"Would you believe I hiked all the way up here to take a selfie for my best friend?" Carmen asked.

"No," Joy said with a laugh.

"Good," Carmen said. "Because it definitely wasn't that."

Joy got up off the snowboard abruptly, and Carmen wondered if she'd said something wrong. It *was* a pretty silly thing to do, and she'd damaged Joy's snowboard because of it. She thought that Joy might be mad, but instead she pulled her phone out of her pocket and crouched down in front of Carmen.

"What are you doing?"

"We're not going to all this trouble and winding up with broken boards and sprained ankles for nothing," she said. "I'll take your picture."

"No," Carmen tried to object, wishing that the snowmobile would just get here already and save her from the most embarrassing moment of her life. But Joy was insistent, and Carmen ended up giving in. Joy crouched low in front of Carmen, framing the mountain in the back of the shot to make it look as large and impressive as possible and when she showed Carmen the photo, she'd done a pretty good job of hiding the fact that Carmen was sitting on her ass in wet jeans instead of skiing down a mountainside. "That's actually really good. Thanks."

"No problem," Joy said, her eyes lingering on Carmen for just a beat too long – or so she thought – before she asked, "What's your number? I'll text it to you and then you'll have it when you get a new phone."

Carmen gave it to her, pulse racing a little faster than it ought to as she wondered if there was any chance that Joy might use that number for anything other than simply sending her a staged selfie. She looked up through her lashes as she asked, "Does Emerald Hill have a phone store?"

NINE

JOY

Snow patrol arrived not long after Joy took Carmen's trophy photograph for her. Instead of a snowmobile it turned out to be two medics on skis, pulling a stretcher shaped like a toboggan behind them through the snow. Carmen groaned the moment she saw it and turned to Joy.

"This is so mortifying," she said. "Are you really going to make me ride down the mountain on a stretcher?"

"I won't," Joy said with a sympathetic look. "But they might."

She knew the resort's policies, and since she'd needed to call the medics there was no way Carmen would be getting off the mountain without a ride in the stretcher. One of the medics took a look at Carmen's ankle and confirmed that it really was just a sprain, and the other asked Joy, "Are you hurt, too?"

"No," she said. "But my board's broken."

"We could give you a lift, but we'd have to make a second trip for you," he said, and she shook her head.

"Nah, don't worry about it," she said. "I'll figure it out."

She watched as the medics got Carmen tucked into the stretcher, amid her protests that she wasn't nearly injured enough to need to be immobilized.

"They have to," Joy explained to her. "Resort policy, it's not safe for you to ride on the stretcher unless they strap you down."

"Great," Carmen said with a little laugh. "Just what I need to make the humiliation complete."

"On the contrary," Joy said. "You look like a badass, like Hannibal Lecter in that scene where they're transporting him from the prison, only lying down."

"Oh yeah, that's exactly the mental image that I want you to have of me," Carmen said. "Criminally insane cannibal is so much better than idiot trying to get a selfie."

"I don't think you're an idiot," Joy said, and then the medics picked up the handles of the stretcher and prepared to take Carmen down the mountain.

"Could you please just take me straight to my cabin?" she asked them. "It's number four."

"Sure," they said.

Joy grabbed her broken binding and her snowboard, slipping her boot back into the remaining intact binding. She figured she could probably make it down the mountain using the snowboard as if it were a skateboard, as long as she took it slow. It was lucky that this had happened on one of the more gradual hills, or else she'd be walking down.

"Hey wait," she said to the medics, testing out the skateboard method as she shoved off and glided over to the stretcher. She grinned at Carmen when she got there, dropping to the snow to make for a gentle stop. "You want to make yourself useful since you're just lying there?"

"Yeah," Carmen said with a smirk, and Joy tucked the broken binding into the bottom of the stretcher, careful to avoid her injured ankle.

"Hold onto that for me," she said. "I'm going to have my work cut out for me trying to board with only one binding, I don't need luggage too."

"Thanks," Carmen said, rolling her eyes. "I feel so helpful."

"You're welcome," Joy said, and then emboldened by the depths of Carmen's eyes, she winked. "See you at the bottom."

TEN

CARMEN

The trip down the mountain was much quicker than hiking up it, and Carmen focused her attention on Joy as the medics slowly brought her down the hill. She was pretty securely strapped down to the stretcher, with not a lot of room to move, but she could see Joy gliding along on her snowboard in the periphery of her vision.

She had noticed that Joy was pretty last night, but she didn't give much thought to her because it was rare that she'd come into repeated contact with the same employee in a resort as big as this. Now, though, she wondered what that wink was all about. Was it just a friendly gesture, or was it possible that Joy had the same fire burning inside her that Carmen had felt when they shared a seat on the snowboard?

The medics made good time getting her back to the cabin, and she was grateful that Joy followed them all the way there, stepping off her snowboard and walking beside the stretcher when they got closer. Carmen still had her broken binding wedged between her feet, and she was trying to think of something clever to say to Joy when they got back to the cabin – something probing but which wouldn't be too personal or too embarrassing to say in front of the medics.

She drew a blank by the time they came to a stop in front of the cabin door, but it didn't matter because the cold from her wet jeans had set in during the journey and she was shivering so hard that her teeth were chattering and she wouldn't have been able to pull off a flirtatious inquiry if she'd wanted to. The medics bent down to free Carmen from the stretcher and she handed Joy her binding.

"Are you sure you don't want to come to the lodge and have the resort nurse take a look at your ankle?" one of the medics asked, and Carmen shook her head.

"It's just a sprain," she said. "Thanks for your help."

"It's what we're here for," he said. Carmen took a tentative step toward the cabin, limping as she put the majority of her weight on her uninjured leg, and Joy came over and looped Carmen's arm around her shoulder.

"Come on," she said. "I'll help you get comfortable."

"Thanks," Carmen said, her heart in her throat once again and her teeth chattering lightly.

The medics headed back to the lodge and Joy helped Carmen limp into the cabin. It was still early – the large clock above the kitchen sink telling her it was a little past noon – and the cabin was empty. Her family would be enjoying their sushi lunch about now, and it was a good thing Carmen texted her mother before she left this morning because she had no way of communicating with them now.

"You're shivering," Joy said as she kicked the door shut behind her and dropped her broken binding on the floor so she could better hold up Carmen. "You'd better get out of those wet jeans before you get sick."

Carmen nodded, then pointed Joy down the hall to the last bedroom. "Can you help me get to my room so I can find some dry clothes?"

"Yeah, of course," Joy said, her voice going a little bit huskier as she helped Carmen slowly down the hallway. "This bedroom?"

"Yeah."

Joy helped Carmen sit down on a vanity chair near the window, then Carmen said, "Can you go into that black bag over there and find me a pair of leggings and a sweater?"

"Sure," Joy said. Carmen took off her jacket, hanging it over the back of the chair, while Joy sat down on the floor and unzipped the suitcase. She sorted through a pile of carefully folded clothes, finding a pair of gray, fleece-lined leggings and an oversized burgundy sweater. "These good?"

"Yeah," Carmen said, taking them as Joy handed them to her. "Thanks."

"Umm," Joy said, hesitating. "Do you need help?"

"No," Carmen said with a smile. "I don't think I'm that much of an invalid."

"Okay, I'll wait in the hall," Joy said.

She stepped out of the room, but getting changed turned out to be a harder task than Carmen expected. Her ankle had swollen a bit more since the last time she'd looked at it on the slopes, and it hurt to take her boot off.

Once that was done, she had to struggle out of her wet jeans, which clung to her and put up quite a fight. Just as she managed to free herself from them, wincing as she pulled them over her swollen ankle, she heard Joy knock on the door frame.

"Oh shit," she said, looking away from Carmen in her underwear. "I'm sorry."

She was holding a towel in her hand and she put one hand in front of her eyes.

"I thought you'd need a towel," she explained.

"That would be helpful, actually," Carmen said. "It didn't occur to me how miserable it would be to mix denim with snow."

"Yeah, we've got to get you some appropriate ski wear before you go back out there," Joy said. She tossed the towel across the room and Carmen caught it, then she went back into the hallway.

Carmen dried off and got dressed, smiling all the while at the use of the word 'we'. It seemed increasingly possible that Joy was interested in her in more than a professional capacity, and Carmen liked the idea of flirting with Joy a little bit and testing the waters.

"Okay," she called. "I'm decent."

Joy came back into the room and Carmen put her arm around her shoulder again, hopping on her good foot while Joy helped her back into the living room. She eased her into an overstuffed lounge chair by the fireplace, picking up Carmen's bad ankle gingerly and putting it on the ottoman in front of the chair.

"You'll want to keep that elevated," she said. Carmen nodded and an involuntary shiver ran through her. She'd been in those wet clothes for so long that she felt chilled to the bone, and it'd probably take a long time to get warm. Joy noticed and asked, "Still cold?"

"Yeah," she said, and Joy went over to the coffee table, grabbing a remote control to turn on the gas fireplace. Flames jumped into view and Joy dialed them down to a comfortable level.

"Good?" she asked. Carmen nodded and Joy followed up with, "How's the ankle?"

"Not great," she admitted. "But I'll live. Umm, do you want to stay a little while?"

Carmen hadn't had a lot of experience with flirtation, or women for that matter, and her pulse was pounding in her ears as she waited for Joy's response. She glanced at the clock in the kitchen and said, "I have to start work in an hour and a half, but I'll stay for a bit."

"You don't have to," Carmen added quickly.

"No, I want to," Joy said. "Where's your family, anyway?"

"Denver," Carmen said. "Shopping."

"Oh," Joy said. "You didn't want to go with them?"

"Not really," Carmen said with a shrug, another shiver rolling up her spine and vibrating outward. The heat from the fireplace was nice, but the cold had gone deep into her. "It's not really my scene."

"You're still freezing," Joy said. She went over to the couch and pulled a knit lap blanket off the back of it, and this time she didn't toss it to Carmen like she'd done with the towel. She came over to the lounge chair and tucked her in, and all the while Carmen was sure her heart might stop beating all together. Joy looked up to see Carmen watching her, her tongue flicking out of her mouth and gliding over her lower lip for just a second, and then she stood upright again. "Do you like hot cocoa?"

"Who doesn't like hot cocoa?" Carmen asked, wishing she'd been brave enough to do something like taking Joy's hand or pulling her onto the chair with her.

"Good answer," Joy said, going over to the kitchen island. "Have you tried the mix here yet? It's out of this world."

Carmen told her that she hadn't – they'd gone to the steakhouse last night and she had her fill of dessert at the restaurant, so none of them had a chance to dig into the welcome basket left by the resort. Even Carmen's sugar fiend sisters hadn't gotten around to it yet, but she made a mental note to recommend the hot cocoa to them when they got back.

For now, she watched Joy retrieving a pair of mugs from the upper cabinets, then a saucepan from beneath the island. She went to the refrigerator and took out a bottle of milk, asking, "Is it okay if I use this?" and Carmen told her it was fine. Her mother had ordered the groceries that were in the fridge and she doubted Mom would miss a little milk.

While Joy heated it on the stove and then mixed in the cocoa powder, Carmen asked, "So what do you do here at the resort?"

"A little bit of everything," Joy said. "I'm a shift supervisor, so I basically just do whatever needs doing."

"Including rescuing girls off the side of the mountain," Carmen said, laughing at herself.

"That was a new one for me," Joy said, smirking at Carmen. "Are you going to learn how to ski for real on this trip, or just continue faking your selfies?"

"I don't know," Carmen answered. "You'd have to ask my dad – he's the one with the itinerary."

Joy laughed, then carefully poured the finished hot cocoa into the mugs she'd gotten out. She brought them both over to where Carmen was sitting, handing her one and then walking over to the Christmas tree in front of the picture window. Carmen craned her head to watch as Joy plucked a couple of candy canes off the tree, then came over and sat down on the edge of the large ottoman. Carmen tried to move her foot out of the way, wincing slightly, and Joy gestured for her to leave it.

She unwrapped both candy canes and then leaned forward, dropping one of them into Carmen's mug with a look that seemed like a challenge. There was very little doubt left in her mind that Joy was interested in her, and Carmen felt her pulse in her ears as she summoned all of her courage to make sure Joy knew it was mutual. She retrieved the candy cane and kept her eyes locked on Joy as she licked the hot cocoa from it.

"Thank you," she said, and Joy's eyebrows raised almost imperceptibly, her teeth sinking into her lower lip just for a second.

Then Carmen's courage melted away and she dropped the candy cane back into her mug, taking a sip while Joy sat there watching her, stirring her own candy cane slowly in her mug. "You're welcome."

"Oh wow," Carmen said as she lowered her cup. "That is incredible. I don't know if it's the chocolate or the milk – I've never had hot cocoa with milk in it – but it's really delicious."

"What?" Joy asked, furrowing her brows. "You've never had hot cocoa with milk? *That's* the part you're impressed by?"

"Yeah," Carmen said, and she had to laugh at how utterly shocked Joy looked.

"How is that possible?"

Carmen shrugged.

"I'm usually a coffee or tea kind of girl. I don't think I've had hot cocoa since I was a kid, and back then we were kinda poor." That was putting it mildly, but there was no reason to give this practical stranger a complete history of the Castillo family's rise from the gutters. She added, "My mom always just used water to save money."

Joy curled her lip in disgust. "Gross. Wasn't it all watered down?"

"Probably," Carmen said, laughing. "But I didn't know any better. What about you? Did you grow up here, drinking amazing hot cocoa and having the most magical Christmases ever?"

"Well, I did grow up here," Joy said. "And it is pretty magical in the wintertime."

"But?" Carmen asked. Joy's mood had shifted into a slightly melancholy tone.

"It just gets a little lonely living in a town where so much of the population is made up of seasonal visitors," she said. "It feels like there's not a whole lot of permanence sometimes. Most of my high school friends have moved away and my own mother moved to Florida a couple years back."

"Aww, that's sad," Carmen said, getting up the nerve to put her hand on top of Joy's. It was warm and the way that Joy rubbed her thumb over the side of Carmen's hand sent little sparks through her. After a minute, though, she snapped out of it.

"I'm sorry," she said, pulling away and taking a sip of her cocoa. "My mom moved because the cold was hell on her joints, and I'm not nearly as pathetic as I just made myself sound. So tell me, what does your family usually do for Christmas? Do you vacation every year?"

"Yeah, but usually we go somewhere with a warm climate. My mom's favorite is Cancun so that's usually where we go," Carmen said. "This year, I think my dad wanted my younger sisters to see what it was like to have a snowy Christmas before they got too old to be amazed by it."

"You're never too old for that," Joy said. Then she nodded to the picture window behind Carmen. "Look."

JOY

Carmen twisted around in her seat again and saw that it had begun to snow. Large, fluffy flakes were falling outside, and the sun shone so brightly that the snow that blanketed the ground was sparkling like someone had dusted it with glitter. She wondered if her family was somewhere that would allow them to see this – it was exactly what her dad had been seeking when he booked this vacation, and it would be a shame if they missed it.

"Beautiful," she breathed. She watched the snow come down for a minute or two, and when she turned back around, Joy was watching her with a spark of desire in her eyes.

ELEVEN

JOY

There was something about this girl... Joy couldn't tear her eyes away.

She set her mug down on the end table next to the chair and Carmen slowly did the same. It felt like all the air had suddenly been sucked out of the room, and the way Carmen was looking at her, she was filling it back up with an electric charge. Joy leaned forward on the ottoman, putting her hands on the arms of the lounge chair while her heart thrummed out an anxious beat in her veins.

If she was reading this moment wrong, she'd probably have to answer some pretty uncomfortable questions for her manager. But it certainly didn't feel wrong.

Carmen leaned forward and Joy knelt on the ottoman, mindful of her ankle as she bent down to kiss her. Their lips met, Joy's eyes closing just as a burst of shivery pleasure ran through her. Carmen's plump lips felt even better than she'd imagined, and she tasted like cocoa and peppermint.

Joy let out a satisfied little sigh, then pulled back for a moment to study Carmen and retreat if necessary.

Instead, Carmen put her hands on either side of Joy's face, warm from the cocoa mug, and pulled her back in. Joy dropped to her knees in front of the lounge chair to get closer to her, and ran one hand through Carmen's hair – thick and soft as silk. It smelled like fresh flowers and Joy had the sudden urge to bury her face in it. Everything about Carmen was delicate and alluring, soft and intoxicating.

She opened her mouth and Carmen did the same, their tongues meeting tentatively, and then a little more urgently. Carmen's hands traveled down from Joy's cheeks, gently tracing the curve of her jaw and then gliding over her neck and tangling in her short hair. She pulled Joy closer and, emboldened, Joy wrapped her arms around Carmen, coaxing her closer to the edge of the chair. Her waist was small, the feel of her curves against Joy's hands causing the blood to rush back into her cheeks.

And just as she was tightening her grip, pulling Carmen to her, Joy heard the front door bang open. The rest of the Castillos burst into the cabin in a cacophony of conversations and rustling shopping bags, and Joy practically leaped up from the floor, whirling around to face them with her heart pounding for a whole new reason.

"Hi, honey," Mrs. Castillo said to Carmen, and when she noticed Joy standing there, she didn't miss a beat. She said, "Oh, good. Would you mind stopping whatever you're doing to help with the bags?"

Relief washed over Joy – Mrs. Castillo thought she was here on resort business, not getting to first base with her daughter. Joy was more than happy to perpetuate that belief, so she rushed over to take the shopping bags she had lined up both arms.

"Thank you. Could you please put them on the dresser in the master bedroom?" Mrs. Castillo asked, and then she got a look at Carmen with her foot propped up and swollen on the ottoman. "What happened to you, baby?"

"What's the matter?" Mr. Castillo said, going over to Carmen while the twin girls went ahead of Joy down the hall to their room to unload their own new purchases. Joy shot a mirthful look at Carmen over her dad's shoulder, and Carmen quickly mouthed the word 'sorry' to her, then launched into the explanation of her mountainside adventure for her parents' sake.

"I went to check out the ski slopes, but the mountain got the better of me," she said. "I fell and twisted my ankle, and I lost my phone, too."

Joy noticed with a smirk that Carmen omitted the part about their collision, as well as the part about hiking her way up a hill in pursuit of a selfie. She couldn't blame Carmen – she probably would have said something similar if their roles were reversed – and she went down the hall to unload Mrs. Castillo's bags. There were a half-dozen of them, all from designer stores, and Joy lined them up neatly on top of the dresser as she'd been instructed.

When she got back to the living room, Carmen's mom was fussing over her ankle, propping pillows beneath it to elevate it higher, and her dad was calling down to the resort to ask for a couple ice packs. Joy tried to be casual as she made her way to the door, calling to no one in particular, "Okay, well if you need anything else don't hesitate to call the desk."

Carmen waved at her, giving her a slightly disappointed look, and Joy knew exactly how she felt. She would have loved to stay in that moment alone in the cabin with her a while longer, but it was probably a good thing the Castillos were home now – her shift was starting in just a couple of minutes. Mr. Castillo hung up with room service and rushed over to Joy, meeting her at the door.

"Hold on a second," he said, pulling his wallet out of his back pocket.

"Oh, that's not necessary–"

"Of course it is," he said. "Thanks for all your help, with the bags and with Carmen's injury."

"Umm..." Carmen was smirking at her from the lounge chair as her dad pressed a twenty-dollar bill into Joy's hand. She felt guilty taking the money, but it would have seemed strange if she had refused. "Thanks."

She figured she could always give it back to Carmen the next time she saw her – whenever that would be. Joy stuffed the bill into the pocket of her ski pants and then grabbed her coat and left before anything more awkward could happen.

※

THE RESORT WAS a little quieter that evening. Joy was used to the mayhem of the day shift, especially this close to Christmas, but people usually went into town for dinner or spent the evening whiling away the hours in front of the fireplaces in the lodge. It made for an easy shift, and Joy was glad for it because after her eventful morning, she was surprisingly tired.

Her mind kept drifting back to two points – the kiss, of course, and the stuff she'd told Carmen about her mom and her friends all moving away. Obviously, she was upset about the likelihood of Danny making Memphis his new home, but Joy wasn't really the type to share sad details of her life with strangers – was she really that torn up about it that she had to vent to pretty girls with twisted ankles that turned them into captive audiences? Irritated, yes – she still hadn't received so much as a text message from him – but not torn up.

Joy got back to the apartment a little after midnight, her eyelids already feeling heavy and begging for sleep, but instead of going to bed, she turned on the Christmas tree lights and used her phone to play some instrumental Christmas music. She lay down on the couch and watched the lights twinkle on the tree, flickering on and off and casting the dark room in alternating reds and blues, yellows and greens. It was her favorite way to fall asleep when she was a kid – every night except for Christmas Eve, of course, or Santa wouldn't come. Without Danny in the apartment to call her a weirdo, Joy figured she might as well sleep in the company of the Christmas tree tonight.

She would have to call her mom tomorrow, during her lunch break or after work. They talked a few times a week usually, and sometimes less when Joy got caught up with the holiday rush at work. They'd already shipped their Christmas gifts to each other and Joy's was wrapped and sitting under her tree. When her mom moved to Florida they'd started a tradition of video calling each other on Christmas morning to exchange gifts since it was impossible for Joy to get away from the resort at that time of year and impractical for her mother to come back to Colorado just to have a rheumatism flare-up. Joy knew she would see her mom in a couple of weeks when she took vacation, but tonight she was missing her.

She had just about drifted off to sleep with visions of Carmen's plump lips and smoldering eyes dancing in her head when the music cut out and her phone began to vibrate on the coffee table.

Joy grabbed it, wondering if her mom's parent sense had kicked in – it happened often enough to be a little crazy, but this time it was Danny.

Finally.

"Finally!" Joy said as she answered the call. "Where the hell have you been?"

"We just finished our first show," he said. He sounded like he was on cloud nine, and there was a lot of noise in the background – like they had *literally* just finished the show. "Joy, it was *incredible*. I can't even describe it, being on-stage with The Hero's Journey."

Joy smiled, and a lot of her anger at Danny's utter lack of communication melted away. She had a hard time staying mad at people. "That's really cool. Is there video of it somewhere so I can watch you?"

"Yeah, I'm sure it'll get posted on the band's social media feeds," he said, and she interrupted him.

"*Your* band's social media feeds."

"Not yet," Danny said. "But I think they really like me."

"Told you," Joy said. She sat up to talk to him and a slight twinge shot through her neck. It had been getting progressively stiffer all evening, and she wondered if she had gotten a mild case of whiplash from the accident. The collision had been hard enough that it was certainly possible. She massaged her neck while Danny gushed to her about the band, the music, and the fans.

"It's going to be an absolutely insane couple of weeks," he said. "We've got shows booked almost every night, from Memphis to Maine."

"Wow," Joy said. "They're keeping you busy, that's for sure."

"Definitely," he answered. "Sorry I didn't call you yesterday – I went straight from the plane into rehearsal and it was an insane day. How's everything at the resort?"

"Pretty good," Joy said.

She was thinking about how Carmen's hands felt when they had run over the same part of her neck, the electricity that her fingers had sent through Joy's body. She wondered for a second about telling Danny about Carmen. Joy remembered the comment he'd made at the airport about finding a girlfriend, and she knew he'd be delighted at this development even if it was just a holiday fling. Hell, for all Joy knew it had been an isolated incident.

She decided not to mention it, and then her mouth betrayed her and she said, "I met a girl today."

"Really?" Danny said, and he was *almost* more enthusiastic about this than he was about the band.

Joy rolled her eyes and said, "Yes."

"How did that happen?"

"I, uhh, ran into her on the slopes," she said with a smirk that Danny could not see.

"Oh yeah? Is she a skier or a snowboarder?" he asked.

"Neither," Joy said. "She was hiking and I literally ran into her with my snowboard, sprained her ankle."

"Oh wow," Danny said, and Joy could tell he was laughing at her but trying to hide it. "And she still wanted to talk to you after that? Or is this, like, an admiring from afar kind of situation?"

"No, we talked," Joy said. She felt a blush rising into her cheeks as she thought again about the kiss, and that was a detail she really would keep to herself. But she felt compelled to tell Danny the most mortifying part about the whole experience. She said, "I helped her get down off the mountain, took her back to her cabin, and then her dad tipped me twenty bucks."

"Win-win," Danny joked.

"It was mortifying," Joy said, and then the volume of whatever was going on in the background where Danny was intensified.

"Hey, I gotta go," he said. "Talk to you soon?"

"Yeah, hopefully," Joy said. "Have fun on tour."

"Thanks," he said, and then he added, "Have fun with your new friend. If it gets serious we may have to tell my mom that we're finally splitting up."

Joy laughed and they hung up, and then she was all alone in the apartment again, the lights on the Christmas tree alternating faithfully from red to blue, yellow to green, and back again.

DECEMBER 19

TWELVE

CARMEN

Carmen woke up early the next morning to pain throbbing in her ankle. She peeled back her heavy blanket and saw that her ankle had swollen to about twice its normal size in the night. She winced as she attempted to flex her foot and found it rather stiff. The ice pack she'd gone to bed with was soggy and warm, so she got up and half limped, half hopped her way into the kitchen for another one.

Room service had brought about six of them to the cabin when Dad called yesterday – overkill for a single twisted ankle, Carmen thought – along with a bottle of Advil to help with the swelling and pain. She grabbed an ice pack and limped into the living room to apply it to her ankle.

The sun was just beginning to rise over the mountain and Carmen lay down on the couch facing the picture window so she could watch the oranges and pinks of the changing sky. It looked like it had snowed again overnight, the ground outside the cabin coated in perfectly clean, unmarred snow. After a few minutes, the sky outside growing increasingly beautiful, she heard someone come into the room behind her, and then her mother's voice.

"Hey, honey," she said. "I thought I heard someone get up."

"I needed a new ice pack," Carmen said.

Mom came over and sat at the other end of the couch, inspecting the swelling. "Poor girl, it looks worse than yesterday. You want some Advil?"

"Yeah," Carmen said. "Please."

She got up and Carmen kept watching the sunrise, her eyes feeling heavy with sleepiness still. Her dreams last night had been filled with Joy, and she'd spent a long time last night wondering how she could get another moment with her like they'd had on the lounge chair. Her lips had been so inviting, so thrilling. Another meet-cute collision on the slopes was out of the question, but maybe Carmen could steal a few minutes of Joy's time if she found her at the lodge later today.

Mom came back a few minutes later holding a plate with a cranberry scone, a glass of orange juice, and the Advil bottle. Carmen took it gratefully and Mom sat down on the ottoman across from her, looking out the window. "This place has some really spectacular views. Don't tell your father, but it might be better than Cancun."

Carmen let out a mocking gasp, then laughed and said, "Yeah, there's a lot of genuine beauty out here."

She was finishing her scone, the sky growing lighter outside, when Dad came into the living room, tying a plush, resort-issue robe tight around his waist. He went into the kitchen to brew a pot of coffee and called to Carmen and Mom, "You two are up early. Excited about the dog sleds?"

"Oh, is that today?" Carmen asked. Joy had taken such a prominent place in her mind since yesterday that she'd completely forgotten about the items on Dad's meticulously planned itinerary.

"She can't go with her ankle like this," Mom said, and Carmen hated to see how Dad's face fell instantly.

"It's that bad?"

"It's swollen," Mom said. "Look at it."

Dad came over and Mom lifted the ice pack momentarily so he could see just how bad Carmen's ankle was, and she said, "I'm sorry, Daddy."

"It's not your fault, kid," he said, standing with his hand over his chin for a minute, thinking. "Well, the dog sled excursions are booked solid so I can't reschedule or we won't get to go at all. You sure you can't tough it out? You're just going to be sitting in the sled the whole time."

"There's a lot of walking to get there, honey," Mom said. "And I can't imagine the sled ride is particularly smooth – I just don't want her to be in pain the whole time."

"Alright," Dad said with a sigh. "I'll go cancel it."

"No," Carmen objected. "You should still go. I'll be okay by myself one more day."

In the back of her mind, she thought a little bit selfishly that it would make for a good opportunity to try and reconnect with Joy. Maybe she could call down to the front desk and make up an excuse for her to come to the cabin for a little while.

"I can stay here with you," Mom offered, but Dad looked crestfallen. This was supposed to be his big, festive family vacation and Carmen had ruined his plans the first two days in a row. She felt guilty, and she wasn't going to ruin her mother's vacation as well.

"I'll be fine," she said. "I just need to rest and ice my ankle – I don't need you here for that."

She wasn't sure which was worse – telling her dad that she wasn't going to participate in another one of his itinerary items, or telling her mom that she didn't need her. Carmen decided to shut her mouth before she dug herself in even deeper.

"Okay," Mom said. "Well, I'll get you set up with whatever you need before we leave. Then when we get back, we'll order lunch and watch a Christmas movie."

❄

CARMEN'S FAMILY headed out a couple hours later for their dog sledding excursion. For once, Marisol and Maria didn't have their phones or tablets glued to their hands. Instead, they were talking excitedly about the dog kennel tour that would immediately precede the sledding – they were more eager to pet the dogs than be pulled through the snow by them. Dad tried one last time to get Carmen to come along, but Mom told him to stop pestering her, then brought the television remote and the mystery novel she'd been reading on the plane in case Carmen got bored.

"Here," Mom said, handing Carmen her phone as well. "If you need anything, call Dad."

Then they were gone and Carmen was alone in the cabin again.

It was just a little after nine in the morning and Carmen thought it would seem too eager, or too forward, to call the front desk and try to ask for Joy so early in the day. The snow started falling again outside, light, delicate flakes floating peacefully down to the earth, and Carmen thought about her sisters, probably having the time of their lives with Husky puppies. She tried to pass the time with the television, but nothing really grabbed her attention.

Ordinarily, she'd be using this time to catch up with Brigid, looking at all the vacation photos her other friends were posting online and crafting the perfect status message to go with her own Colorado mountain photographs. But Carmen's phone was buried in a snow-drift somewhere on the slope called Outer Limits, and she couldn't get her mind off Joy. She even tried the mystery novel Mom left her, but it wasn't long before she started to feel stir-crazy alone in the cabin and confined to the couch.

Fortunately when she got up to limp her way to the bathroom, she discovered that the Advil really had taken the swelling in her ankle down quite a bit. It was almost back to its normal size and not nearly so tender as it had been this morning. She could even put a little bit of weight on it, which helped as she made her way across the cabin.

On her way back, Carmen caught sight of the broken binding of Joy's snowboard sitting just inside the foyer. She must have forgotten it in her haste to leave after the rest of the Castillos came home, and Carmen had fibbed, telling her parents that it was a part of her ski which had broken in the accident. There was no real reason to keep her kiss with Joy a secret – her parents knew she'd been with girls before – but the way they'd come home and immediately assumed that Joy was there to be utilized as a resort employee had made it awkward to tell them the truth.

Now, though, Carmen smiled as she saw the broken binding as an opportunity. She'd been wondering how to reach out to Joy, thinking it would be absolutely ridiculous to call down to the resort's front desk and ask for her. All she'd come up with so far was something crazy like, *Hey, I was thinking about that amazing kiss we shared yesterday, and I was wondering if you want to do it again?* But the binding offered a perfectly logical excuse to talk to her again.

Carmen sat down in the lounge chair and picked up the resort phone sitting on the end table beside it. She dialed the front desk and asked the man who answered, "Is Joy available? Umm, I don't know her last name."

"Turner," he said. "I think she's in the bar area – just give me a minute."

He put her on hold and butterflies started fluttering

in Carmen's stomach while she listened to a soft, slow guitar rendition of White Christmas. Then the music abruptly cut out and she heard Joy's voice. "This is Joy, how can I help you?"

"Umm," Carmen said as she realized that she hadn't given the front desk attendant her name or a reason for her call, and now for a moment she was frozen, the butterflies taking over her mind as well as her belly. Then she snapped out of it and said, "Hi, this is Carmen Castillo."

"Oh, hey," Joy said, her voice immediately switching over from crisp and professional to friendly, and Carmen was relieved. In the back of her mind she'd been fearing all this time that their kiss had meant more to her than it did to Joy, and that it might not be something she cared to think twice about. She asked, "How's your ankle today?"

"A lot better, actually," Carmen said. "It hurt like hell this morning, but some Advil and an ice pack took the swelling down. I did have to skip this morning's dog sledding excursion, though."

"Oh no, are you all alone again?" Joy asked.

"I am," Carmen said. "Just til lunchtime."

"You're having a rough vacation," Joy said, sympathy dripping in her voice.

"I wouldn't say that. Some parts have been pretty nice," Carmen was quick to interject. Then she remembered the reason for her call, or at least the pretense. "Oh, I've got your broken snowboard binding. You left it in my cabin."

"Oh yeah," Joy said. "Well, I'm kinda swamped at the

bar right now, but I could come by later and pick it up if that's okay."

Carmen was disappointed – she'd really been hoping to see Joy now, but of course she had work to do. She asked, "What if I bring it to you?"

"Are you feeling up to it?"

"Sure," Carmen said. "Besides, I've barely gotten to check out the lodge so far."

"Well come on over then," Joy said. "I'm in the bar area stocking liquor, but they're obligated by law to give me a break pretty soon. I could give you the tour."

Carmen hung up the phone with a stupidly large grin on her face. She tried not to think about how her dad would feel if he knew that she'd skipped his planned activity just to go continue her flirtation with Joy, but how was Carmen to know that her ankle would make a miraculous recovery after a hearty dose of ibuprofen? She limped back down to her bedroom and put on a little bit of makeup, then a pair of black leggings and a soft, oversized flannel shirt, along with her boots and coat which had dried out overnight.

Her boot fit a little snugly over her twisted ankle and Carmen winced as she pulled it on, then went back into the kitchen to get a fresh ice pack out of the freezer to take with her. It was the last thing she wanted squished down the side of her boot – because of the discomfort and also the cold – but she knew it'd help so she did it. Then she called the resort transport van to take her to the lodge, feeling silly on account of the fact that it was a two or three-minute walk from the cabin, but with her limp it would have taken longer.

❄

WHEN CARMEN ARRIVED at the lodge, it was about ten a.m. and the early hour didn't seem to be dampening the spirits of the crowd lounging in the bar area. The room was large and open, with lots of tables, plush armchairs, and several wood-burning fireplaces spaced throughout the room where people could come and warm themselves after coming in off the slopes.

That's what a lot of them appeared to be doing – warming up after a run, or fortifying themselves before they went out to conquer the mountain – and Carmen thought this would be a perfectly cozy place to while away an afternoon. The logs crackled in fireplaces all around the lounge, she could smell spiced apple cider and cinnamon, and best of all, she spotted Joy behind the bar. She was standing on a step ladder, stocking high-end whisky bottles on the highest shelves, and when she climbed down to pick up a couple more bottles, she noticed Carmen from across the room.

A genuine smile broke across her lips and Carmen could see warmth in her sapphire eyes even from that distance. She waved at her with the hand holding Joy's snowboard binding, then gestured to one of the armchairs nearby. Joy nodded, and Carmen sat down to wait for her, setting the binding on the seat of a neighboring chair to reserve it.

She finished shelving the whisky bottles and Carmen couldn't tear her eyes off her. Most of the interactions they'd had so far had been hectic – her family checking into the resort with their mountain of luggage, their collision on the slopes, the pounding of blood in her ears as she felt the tension rising between them, and of course, her family bursting into the cabin in the middle of their kiss. It was nice to sit still and watch the world move around Joy.

She seemed unaware of herself in a way that Carmen's New York crowd never was. They always had their phones out, taking selfies, posting messages, checking their makeup and clothes and turning their lives into something to be observed. Carmen had been guilty of that too, and she didn't realize it until she lost her phone and was forcibly removed from that world. But Joy? She was candid and after the few interactions that Carmen had with her, she already knew that Joy was really present in the moment.

The more she watched Joy, the more Carmen realized how deeply she wanted her. She wanted to be close to Joy, and she wanted rather urgently to kiss her again.

Joy moved the empty crate into a back room and then emerged again, locking eyes with Carmen and coming around the end of the bar to meet her. Carmen's heart leapt into her throat.

THIRTEEN

JOY

Joy had been surprised and pleased when she heard Carmen's voice on the phone, and she spent every minute of the time between that call and Carmen's arrival in the lodge anticipating this moment. There was something about this girl that was hard to ignore, even when she tried to keep her mind on her work. It had taken all of her restraint to finish stocking the bar after she saw Carmen, rather than showing just how transparently excited she was to see her by rushing right over to her.

She tried to play it cool, walking casually over to Carmen while her pulse throbbed anxiously in her ears. She was sitting in an armchair, her coat thrown over one arm and the hem of her plaid shirt riding up her thigh in a way that made it difficult for Joy to keep her attention on Carmen's eyes.

Then she noticed the ice pack jammed down the side of Carmen's boot and raised her eyebrows. Joy pointed at it and said, "I thought you were feeling better."

"Better than yesterday," Carmen said. That was about how Joy's neck felt – she'd woken up very stiff, and the more she moved it throughout the morning, the better it felt. Carmen pointed at the empty chair beside her and said, "There's your binding. How much will it cost to repair?"

Joy picked it up and said, "I'll probably have to replace the bindings, but it shouldn't be too expensive. I get an employee discount in the ski shop."

"I'll pay for it," Carmen offered. "It's the least I could do for causing the accident. Just let me know how much it is."

Joy waved the offer away. "I appreciate it, but it's not a big deal. I was probably due for new bindings anyway – that board is about five years old and gets a lot of use."

"Well, if you change your mind-"

"I won't," Joy said with a smile. "Are you still up for a tour? While I was waiting for you I thought of something I think you'll enjoy."

"Sure," Carmen said. She got up and slung her coat over her arm, then took one limping step forward and Joy put her hand out to stop her.

"Is that the best you can walk right now?" she asked. "I'm not going to drag you all over the resort while you pretend not to be in pain."

"But I want the tour," Carmen objected, and Joy gestured her back into the armchair.

"Stay here," she said. "I'll be right back."

She went into the hallway that led to the lobby, walking quickly because she wanted to spend as much of her break as possible with Carmen. She went into a staff-only area behind the front desk and retrieved her coat, then grabbed one of the wheelchairs that were kept there to help mobility-impaired guests to and from their accommodations. When she got back to the lodge, she wheeled it over to Carmen and said, "Your chariot awaits."

Carmen looked from the wheelchair to Joy with incredulity, then asked, "You just love finding ways to embarrass me, don't you?"

Joy grinned and patted the back of the wheelchair, saying, "Just sit down, I don't have all day and I don't want you to hurt your ankle any worse."

"Fine," Carmen said grudgingly, and as she sat in the wheelchair she laughed and said, "I guess this is as close to dog sledding as I'll get today."

"Hey," Joy said. "That makes me the Husky, and I take offense."

"You shouldn't," Carmen said, her cheeks going red as she added, "You're much cuter than the dogs, in my opinion. So where are we going?"

Joy told her it was a secret, then wheeled Carmen out of the lounge. They went past the bank of elevators that led up to the hotel floors, past the lobby with its towering Christmas tree, and all the way down the hallway to a freight elevator. It was for staff use only, but so was the place that Joy was taking Carmen, and she had to take a gamble that everyone else was so busy today no one would notice her smuggling a guest upstairs.

She pushed and held a button on the wall until the elevator came and the doors slid slowly open, and as soon as Carmen saw the industrial, unfinished appearance of the elevator car, she asked with a laugh, "You're going to murder me, aren't you?"

"Nah," Joy said. "Way too many people saw us together in the lodge – it would be foolish to try something like that. I'm taking you to my favorite place in the resort, if you still want to go."

"I'm not crazy about this elevator, but I'll go," Carmen said.

"Yeah, I didn't like it much my first few times riding in it either," Joy said, pushing the wheelchair forward into the elevator car. As she pushed a button to close the door again, she said, "It ain't pretty like the elevator guests use, but in my five years here I've used it almost every day and I can assure you it's safe. And the pay-off at the other end is well worth it."

"Okay," Carmen said. "Let's do it, then."

Joy pushed a button to take them up to the top floor, one that wasn't accessible from the guest-accessible elevators. When they arrived, she opened the doors onto a space that was mainly used for storage. All the resort's Christmas decorations would end up here soon, and Joy would be up and down this elevator a few dozen times bringing down all the New Year's décor. The best part about this space, though, was that it also provided access to a helicopter pad.

In all the time that Joy had worked at the Emerald Mountain Ski Resort, she'd only ever seen it used once, when a guest had sustained a head injury on the slopes and had to be taken to Denver for treatment, but they had to keep the helipad clear of snow and ice just in case it was needed. Joy almost always volunteered for the task because the roof felt so isolated and serene, almost like the feeling of flying down a hill on her snowboard in the early morning or late at night when everyone else had called it quits.

She wheeled Carmen over to the door and told her to put her coat back on, doing the same herself, then she opened the door. Cold air blew in at them, a little flurry of snow cascading into the building from where it had gathered against the door, and Joy heard Carmen suck in a deep, awed breath as she pushed her out to the helipad, stopping in the center of a large letter H painted in the center of it.

The sun was bright and the snow was falling lightly, and Joy made a mental note that she'd need to come back up here and sweep it clear in an hour or two. For now though, she was excited to watch Carmen's reaction to this place. It offered a nearly three hundred and sixty-degree view of the mountain surrounding the resort, and that incredible sight never failed to bring a sense of calm to Joy. She was curious to know if it would have the same effect on Carmen.

"Incredible," she breathed, her mouth hanging open slightly and bringing a smile to Joy's lips.

She stood up so that she could turn around and take in the full view and Joy said, "It really is. I come here as often as I can."

"It's humbling," Carmen said after a minute. She was spinning in a slow circle, delicate snowflakes landing in her hair, and then she stopped and took Joy's hand. "Thank you for showing me this."

"I'm glad you like it," Joy said, lifting Carmen's hand to kiss her fingertips. They were getting cold already and she pulled a pair of gloves out of her pocket, handing them to Carmen. "How do you feel about heights?"

"I'm okay with them," Carmen said, so Joy put her arm around her waist and let Carmen lean on her as she guided her slowly over to the railing at the edge of the roof. Their hips connected as they walked together, and Joy's heart beat a little bit faster, pumping warming blood through her veins.

When they got there, Carmen leaned against the railing to take pressure off her ankle and they looked out over the edge. They were standing directly above the ski area, where all of the slopes converged and the entrances to the lodge and the ski rental area were, only about five stories down. The mountain still managed to loom high above them in the distance, and Carmen let out another awed sigh.

"You're so lucky to live in a place like this," she said. Little skiers and snowboarders the size of train set miniatures cut across the slopes and Carmen watched them, but Joy's eyes were on her. She said, "It reminds me of when I was a kid, only a thousand times prettier and better."

"You mentioned that you grew up poor," Joy said,

hoping that she wasn't prying too much as she asked, "What was that like?"

"We lived in a house just outside of Boston that I've heard my mom classify as a 'hovel,'" Carmen said, smiling. "There was plenty of snow, and it wasn't the slushy, dirty kind that you get in New York City, the stuff that gets run over by cars about a hundred times as soon as it hits the ground. It was really beautiful and I remember spending a lot of my time outside in the winter back then, making snow angels and forts and lobbing my dad with snowballs as soon as he got home from work."

Joy laughed and said, "I think my dad would have belted me for that if I ever tried it."

"Mine only got mad if I didn't have a pile of snowballs ready for him at the end of the driveway so he could return fire," Carmen said. "My little sisters have grown up in a tenth-story penthouse and they associate Christmas with sand instead of snow. I think my dad feels kind of guilty about depriving them of the traditional Christmas experience that I got, even if mine also included IOU's from Santa."

Joy laughed, then looked pityingly at Carmen. "You were really that poor?"

"It wasn't quite that bad," Carmen said, "but we did get pretty desperate for a while. My dad was always good at finding simple things to keep me happy and occupied though."

"Yeah? Like what?" Joy asked.

"Hmm," Carmen said, thinking for a moment, and Joy watched as she bit her lip in the middle of her contemplation. She had to resist the urge to lean over and kiss her in that moment, and then Carmen's eyes lit up. "Oh! When I was around seven years old, I got the *Little House on the Prairie* series from the library and became completely obsessed with it. Have you read them?"

"Of course," Joy said.

"Do you remember the molasses candies they make one Christmas?" Carmen asked, and Joy shook her head. "Well, it basically involved pouring molasses into fresh snow until it froze, or so I thought as a seven-year-old kid. Turns out there must be more to it, but I didn't figure that out until I spent several weeks hounding my dad to buy me molasses so I could try it. I don't know if you've ever bought molasses before, but it's expensive."

"Let me guess," Joy said. "You did not end up with tasty candies."

"No I did not," Carmen said. "He came home one day with a huge smile on his face and pulled a small jar of molasses out of his pocket. This was after he lost his job, so it was a big deal. We immediately found some clean snow to try it on, and I drizzled the entire jar in a big circle in the yard. It was sticky and bitter and it didn't harden at all like in the story. The whole event was over in ten minutes, and my mom got mad that we wasted money pouring molasses all over the yard."

Carmen laughed at the memory, and Joy said, "When I was a kid, my mom would buy me snow cone syrup and I'd pour it over fresh bowls of snow. I bet mine tasted better."

"No doubt," Carmen said, and then Joy couldn't wait any longer. She pulled Carmen into a kiss, long and deep.

Their bulky coats crinkled between them and Carmen's lips and nose were icy with the cold. When she shivered beneath Joy's touch, Joy broke away and brushed an errant snowflake from Carmen's cheek, saying, "We should probably go back inside. You're getting cold, and my break's gotta be over by now."

"Okay," Carmen said, leaning into Joy as she walked her back over to the wheelchair. As they headed back inside, she asked, "Hey, would you want to get drinks or something later?"

"Absolutely," Joy said. "But I can't tonight. I volunteer at a homeless shelter in Emerald Hill once a week and tonight's my night."

"Okay," Carmen said. "Soon, then."

"Of course," Joy answered, calling the elevator and then leaning over to give Carmen one last, long kiss to remember her until they met again.

❄

JOY SPENT the rest of her shift hoping that the time between moments with Carmen wouldn't be too long. From the moment of their kiss yesterday, she was painfully aware of the fact that Carmen would only be in Emerald Hill until the day after Christmas, and the time they had together was limited. It was a shame that the world had to keep turning around her after she looked into those gorgeous eyes.

She even thought about calling Tyler at the shelter and telling him she couldn't come in tonight, but she'd been volunteering there since high school and she knew how badly they needed extra hands during the holidays. So she went, calling her mom on the way over just to check in with her.

"Hi sweetie, what's going on?" she asked as soon as she picked up.

"Not much," Joy lied. She wanted to tell her about Carmen, but she had a feeling that it would sound frivolous if she talked about it out loud – they'd only known each other two days, and the amount of space Carmen was taking up in Joy's mind was not proportionate to that level of familiarity. Instead, she said, "I just wanted to call and see how you're doing in case I get busy with the Christmas rush and we don't talk again this week."

"Oh, I'm good," her mom said. "Your stepdad and I are finally going to get around to checking out Disney World's Christmas displays this weekend."

"That'll be fun," Joy said. Mom and Allan had been saying they wanted to do that since their first year in Florida, but they'd always found an excuse not to go.

"What about you?" Mom asked. "How's life?"

Joy let out a little sigh, and then said, "Life is good. Did you know Danny's touring with The Hero's Journey? One of their guitarists had to drop out of the band unexpectedly so they called him."

"I saw the show videos he was sharing online," Mom said, and Joy realized that she still hadn't had the time to watch them like she promised. She'd do it tonight, after she got done at the shelter.

"He's probably about to get his big break," Joy said, just a little bit of sadness creeping into her voice.

"Are you worried that he'll move away?" Mom asked. She always could tell exactly what Joy was thinking, even through the phone and two thousand miles away.

"I know he will," Joy said. "The band is based in Memphis."

"Maybe it's time for you to move on from Emerald Hill, sweetie," her mom said gently. "You could move east and then you'd be closer to all of us. I'm sure there are lots of opportunities waiting for you out there in the world."

"That's what Danny said," Joy said with a laugh.

Fortunately, she was just pulling into the parking lot of the homeless shelter, so that was a conversation they could save for another time. It was scary to think about uprooting herself and moving away from the only town she'd ever known – she was born here, went to school here, learned to snowboard on Emerald Mountain, had her first kiss, her first girlfriend, her first broken heart here, and her dad was buried in Emerald Hill. There was too much history to just get up and leave like everyone else seemed to do so easily.

She parked her car and said, "Mom, I just got to the shelter so I gotta go, okay?"

"Sure, sweetie," her mom said. "Have a good night."

"Thanks, you too."

"We'll talk on Christmas, alright?"

"Of course," Joy said. "Love you, Mom."

"I love you too, sweetie."

Joy shoved her phone into her pocket and went inside the shelter. It was a small brick building on the outskirts of Emerald Hill, and it served about two dozen homeless, as well as a hundred impoverished families with its food pantry. Joy had been coming here since she learned of its existence during a high school volunteer day in which the kids worked on giving back to the community. She liked giving her time to the shelter because it was the one place in Emerald Hill where impermanence was a good thing. People came here when they were having the worst times in their lives, and the shelter supported them and gave them the tools to get back on their feet. Most of the time when people stopped coming back, it meant they were doing better for themselves.

"Hey," Tyler said, approaching her as soon as Joy arrived.

He was one of the shelter's only full-time staff members, and he was almost always there, coordinating volunteers, working on organizing the food pantry, and helping the shelter's visitors however he could. In the time since Joy started volunteering, she'd watched Tyler go from shy teenager a year above her in school to a jack of all trades, from meal planning to fundraising to resume building. He still got a little harried around the holidays, though, when the shelter was at its busiest.

"How can I help?" Joy asked. It was her go-to line every time she walked through the door, and she asked it even though she was pretty sure she already knew the answer tonight.

"Food pantry needs all the help you can give it," he said. It was a problem every year around the holidays, and Joy was almost always the one who got tapped to try and get a handle on it.

"Sure," she said, then headed into the pantry to get to work.

The room was small, about ten square feet, and every wall was lined from floor to ceiling with shelves of canned goods and non-perishables and personal hygiene items that had been donated to the shelter. Every year around Christmas, the donations reached their peak because of the influx of visitors to Emerald Hill and the resort.

Mostly they were purchased by generous visitors to the resort, but sometimes they came from the vacation homes of people who arrived in Emerald Hill only to realize that they'd forgotten to empty out their pantries before leaving the previous year. They meant well, thinking that the shelter could use their donations, but a lot of these goods were expired, and that left Joy to sort through them all. It was a big project that tended to reach its crisis point around the holidays and Joy didn't mind taking it on.

She tuned into a Christmas music station on her phone, setting it on a high shelf where it wouldn't be in the way, and then she got to work. The first step was weeding out all the expired cans, putting them in a trash bin by the door, and while she did this, Joy liked to take everything down off the shelves, stacking it all in the center of the small room. The influx of donations around the holidays made it hard for already-busy volunteers to organize the canned goods as they came in, and the result was a jumble of cans on every shelf. Joy found it easier to organize them if she just started from scratch.

She was about halfway finished sorting out the expired cans when she heard someone coming into the room behind her. She figured it was Tyler checking in, or a family looking to pick up a few items who had made the unfortunate decision to come while she had the pantry in complete disarray. The last person she expected to find standing in the doorway was Carmen.

"Hey," Joy said, surprised and more than a little pleased. For a moment she wondered if she had gotten so absorbed in her sorting project that she was hallucinating gorgeous girls. "What are you doing here?"

"I thought I'd come and see if you needed an extra hand," Carmen said. She looked at the canned goods stacked in the center of the room and added, "By the looks of it, I'd say that you do."

"Hey, I have a system," Joy said defensively, then she set down the can of creamed corn in her hand and walked over to Carmen, pulling her into a quick kiss. "How did you find me?"

"I googled the shelter," Carmen said with a shrug. "It's the only one in town so it wasn't difficult. I called the resort transport van to bring me here."

"Your family didn't mind you leaving them?" Joy asked.

"Apparently, dog sledding is pretty tiring," Carmen said. "We were going to have a movie night but we made it through *Christmas Vacation* and half of *It's a Wonderful Life* before both of my parents fell asleep on the couch. My sisters were playing some *Harry Potter* game in their room so they'll be glued to their iPads for a couple hours, and I wanted to see you again."

"Well that's sweet," Joy said, tucking a strand of Carmen's hair behind her ear. "I'm just sorting canned goods, though – nothing too exciting."

Carmen was looking around the room, at the stuff stacked on the floor and the nearly-bare shelves. She asked with a smirk, "Are you sure you have a system?"

"Yes, but I never said it was a good one," Joy said. "If you're having second thoughts I wouldn't mind if you just keep me company while I sort cans."

"No," Carmen said. "I've got food pantry experience. I want to help."

"You do?" Joy asked.

"Yeah," Carmen said. "Granted it was on the receiving end of things. We used the pantry in our town a few times after my dad lost his job. So, what are we doing here?"

Joy wanted to ask Carmen how their luck had changed and what series of events led them to stay in one of the resort's luxury cabins, but Carmen changed the subject so abruptly she assumed that the topic was off-limits, at least for the moment. She explained the project to her, telling her that she was working on sorting out the expired goods when Carmen walked in. She wrapped up with her perennial complaint about this project. "I just wish we had a better way of sorting donations as they come in. That's what we do during the rest of the year, but there are so many of them around Christmas time and we're so busy with other things that the pantry gets neglected."

"You definitely need a better system," Carmen said, going over to a shelf and picking up a can to check its expiration date. Joy noticed that she was still favoring her uninjured side, so she went out of the pantry and grabbed a rolling chair from Tyler's office, bringing it back into the room.

"Here," she said, pushing it over to Carmen. "You can do this work sitting down. Don't stress your ankle."

"Thanks," Carmen said, sitting.

She started to scoot away, but Joy grabbed the back of the chair and pulled Carmen back to her. She leaned down and gave her another kiss, longer this time. When she pulled out of it, Carmen was looking at her and those eyes stirred something pleasant and warm in Joy's belly. She said, "Thanks for coming to the shelter. That was a really nice surprise."

FOURTEEN

CARMEN

It took about an hour and a half to finish sorting all the canned goods and put them back on the shelves in some semblance of order, and when they finished, Carmen and Joy took a moment to admire their handiwork. Joy pulled Carmen's chair over to the doorway of the food pantry and they looked at the rows and rows of neatly stacked cans as she said, "We did a good job. Now hopefully it stays this way for more than a day."

Carmen laughed, then stood up so that Joy could return the chair to the office. When she returned, Carmen suddenly felt a little bit nervous, like the room had filled with static charge and what happened next would determine how that energy was expended – whether it dissipated into the air or sent an electric jolt through her body.

Joy asked, "Do you have to go back to the cabin now?"

Carmen's heart was pounding so hard in her chest

she thought it might prevent her from speaking. She'd never felt this strongly about anyone before and Joy had a way of lighting her on fire with a glance. She managed to squeak, "No, I left my parents a note, and I have my mom's phone."

"A note?" Joy asked, and Carmen loved to watch the way her lips curled into a teasing grin. They felt so close to her when they were alone in this little room. Joy asked, "Did you tell them you went to a homeless shelter to meet the girl who twisted your ankle?"

"Not exactly," Carmen said. "I said I was going to the lodge to replenish our hot cocoa supply."

"You know you could have called room service for that," Joy said, her sapphire eyes dancing with amusement.

"I'm not a good liar, okay?" Carmen said. "The point is that my dad will probably be conked out for the night and I've got a little while. What about you?"

"I've got all night," Joy said, and the words brought color to Carmen's cheeks. "Do you want to come over to my apartment? It's not far from here."

"Sure," Carmen breathed, not sure she was capable of more than a single syllable in that moment.

They left the shelter, Joy waving goodbye to her supervisor, and climbed into Joy's car for the short trip to her apartment. Carmen hadn't seen much of Emerald Hill yet. The limousine that drove them from the airport had taken them down the main stretch of town, a mile-long road dotted with shops and restaurants, and her trip from the resort to the shelter had taken place under cover of darkness so aside from a few little cafes and boutiques already closed for the night, there hadn't been much to see out her window. Now, Carmen was far too concerned with what was *inside* the car to pay attention to the town outside it.

She stole glances at Joy the whole way there, anticipating what would happen when they arrived. Carmen had been with a couple other girls, and had a few superficial relationships in college, but none of them had ever evoked the reaction that Joy did every time Carmen was near her. It felt like her heart was in her throat and the fluttering in her stomach filled her with a nervous energy she couldn't wait to expend.

Fortunately, the journey was short, and after just a couple of minutes, Joy pulled into a parking spot in front of a row of townhouses. When they got out of the car, the world felt silent thanks to the darkness and the stillness of the fallen snow. It was only a little past nine o'clock, but it felt much later. For a moment as Joy came around the front of the car and took Carmen's hand, it felt like time itself had stopped.

Then she led Carmen into the apartment, dropping her hand so she could go into the living room and flip a switch on the wall. Instead of a lamp or overhead light, it turned on the sparkling, soft lights of a Christmas tree in the corner, and Joy walked slowly back to Carmen. She was almost a silhouette in the low light, her hips swaying as she walked, and she said as she rejoined Carmen in the entryway, "Welcome to my humble abode."

"It's nice," Carmen said, looking around.

It looked like a place where real people lived, with a well-loved sofa against one wall, some framed movie posters above it, and a small kitchen near the entrance with a rack of dishes drying on the counter. She'd only been here a minute but it already felt cozier and more comfortable than any house Carmen had stayed in over the last ten years, where interior designers dictated everything down to the coffee table décor and everything was too expensive to actually use. Joy's apartment looked like a place where she could sit comfortably and read one of the books on the shelf below the window.

"It's alright," Joy said.

The space between them was quickly narrowing, and Carmen's pulse was racing. There were no elder Castillos to burst in on them now, and she was excited and anxious in a way that made it difficult to separate the two dueling emotions. So she snorted and nodded to the poster above the couch, saying, "I mean, besides the *Die Hard* poster. Do you really like that movie enough to give it pride of place in your living room?"

"No," Joy said. "That belongs to my roommate. I've been trying to get rid of it for years and he just won't budge."

"Oh, thank god," Carmen said, laughing. "I thought I was going to have to leave. So, umm, where *is* your roommate tonight?"

"Memphis," Joy said. Then she stepped forward, her body just barely brushing against Carmen's, and she threaded her fingers into Carmen's hair on either side of her face, pulling her into a kiss. All of Carmen's nervousness melted out of her in that touch, and she let herself sink into Joy.

She put her hands on Joy's hips, squeezing them and aching for her. It had only been a couple of days but the tension building between them made it feel like an eternity. She pulled the zipper of Joy's heavy jacket down, eager to get closer to her. Carmen put her hands inside the jacket, wrapping her arms around Joy's waist and holding her tightly as Joy's tongue found her lower lip and her hips connected with Carmen's.

Joy shimmied her coat down off her shoulders, letting it fall to the floor, and then she did the same to Carmen's coat, pulling it off her and tossing it away. Now that the moment had finally come, the one that had been running like a fantasy through the back of Carmen's mind all evening, they were reduced to a tangle of limbs and heavy breaths and longing.

Joy brought her over to the living area, letting Carmen lean on her to take the weight off her ankle until Joy lowered her to the floor. They kissed, Joy's tongue swiping through her mouth and sending electricity between her thighs while her hands worked at Carmen's clothes.

They undressed each other in a mutual frenzy. Carmen tossed Joy's shirt toward the bookshelf and the sleeve got caught in the branches of the tree, pulling pine needles down on them, and one errant ornament hit Joy squarely on the head.

"Sorry," Carmen said, but Joy was laughing and she

barely paused before yanking Carmen's sweater over her head.

Joy straddled her and leaned down, her warm lips leaving a trail of little fires burning on Carmen's skin everywhere Joy touched her. She kissed her neck, and then her collar bone, tracing a line down the center of her chest while her hands went to the cups of Carmen's bra. Carmen let out a soft moan and put her hands on top of Joy's, pressing them more firmly against her. She could feel desire building between her thighs and she wanted to share every part of herself with Joy.

Joy peeled the straps of Carmen's bra down her arms, lifting her up to unhook it and fling it away. Carmen's nipples stood up in the slight draft from the nearby window and Joy closed her lips around them each in turn, her tongue wetting Carmen's skin and sending shivers of another kind through her.

She reached down to find the buttons of Joy's pants, opening them quickly and putting her hand between her legs. As her palm slid down Joy's stomach and found wetness between her thighs, Joy exhaled shakily and moved her hips against Carmen's hand.

They finished undressing each other, rolling on the floor to pull each other's pants and underwear off and bumping into the tree as little pieces of tinsel fell to the floor around them. Then Joy pushed Carmen onto her back again, their eyes locking for a moment in which Carmen wondered if her heart would ever beat normally again.

Joy crawled slowly between Carmen's thighs, leaving

kisses all across her stomach and over her hips as she went. When she hooked her arms under her thighs, Carmen could feel her breath warm against her skin.

Carmen closed her eyes.

Joy kissed her tenderly at first, exploring her and touching her gently. Then her tongue slid over Carmen's skin and she let out a moan as a warm, wonderful feeling bloomed from her core. Joy's tongue became a little more insistent, teasing and stroking until it felt like her whole body wanted to curl up into a little ball, imploding into the tip of Joy's tongue. They stayed like that for a long time, every stroke of Joy's tongue eliciting another little cry from Carmen's lips, until finally with Joy's lips pressed firmly against her, Carmen tipped over the edge.

She opened her eyes just as a wave of intense pleasure washed over her whole body and saw that she had squirmed her way beneath the tree. All she saw was twinkling lights as Joy's tongue rolled over her and Carmen's body collapsed into a heap of shivering pleasure.

❄

CARMEN STAYED with Joy for as long as she dared, cozying up to her on the couch once the floor finally lost its charm, but around eleven o'clock, her mom called and asked where she was.

"Did you get lost on the way back from the lodge?" she teased, and Carmen looked down at Joy nestled in the crook of her arm.

"No," she said, then fibbed a bit as she explained, "I met a girl and we're just hanging out. I'll be home soon."

It seemed unnecessary to go into every last detail about how she and Joy met, and Carmen still felt a little bit guilty about how important she had become in the midst of a family vacation.

"Okay honey," Mom said. "We're going to bed, but I'll leave a light on for you. Don't be long."

Carmen hung up, then told Joy she had to go back to the cabin. She resolved that tomorrow she'd do whatever it was her family had planned, including whatever was on her dad's detailed itinerary. Joy drove her back to the resort, and it turned out to be rather difficult to get out of her car – Carmen wanted nothing more than to snuggle up and fall asleep next to Joy. Between her busy shifts at the resort and Dad's itinerary, Carmen wasn't sure when she'd get to see Joy again. They shared a lingering kiss and then she went inside.

The cabin was quiet, the kitchen light left on just like her mom had promised, and Carmen went straight into her room and collapsed into bed, letting out a contented sigh and thinking of Joy as she closed her eyes.

DECEMBER 20

FIFTEEN
CARMEN

Carmen woke up the next morning feeling more invigorated and energized than she had since arriving at the resort. That was the point of a vacation, and fresh mountain air, but Carmen supposed that Joy had even more to do with her soaring spirits.

She got out of bed and noticed that her ankle was feeling a lot better, too. It was nearly back to its normal size and it didn't hurt to put pressure on it anymore. She went into the bathroom and took a hot shower, got dressed, and then waited for the rest of her family to get up and seize the day with her.

They all trickled out to the kitchen in their own time, getting mugs of coffee or hot cocoa and then sitting around the island to drink them. They'd finished off the scones after dinner last night, so once everyone was dressed, Carmen suggested they go into Emerald Hill for breakfast.

"I saw a cute little café on Main Street last night," she said. "I bet they have a good breakfast menu."

Dad raised an eyebrow at her and asked, "You went into Emerald Hill?"

"Yeah," Carmen said, a little bit of color coming into her cheeks. Her parents weren't the type that she felt the need to hide things from, but that didn't mean it would be anything less than awkward to explain her fledgling relationship with Joy while the whole family sat around the kitchen island and stared at her. Besides, she'd been hoping to avoid admitting to Dad that instead of participating in his itinerary items, she'd ended up spending that time with a girl. She tried to play dumb, asking, "Didn't Mom tell you?"

"She said you were hanging out with someone," he said. "I assumed you meant in the lodge."

"No, she lives in town," Carmen said. There was no getting out of this now, so she explained "Do you remember the girl that brought us to the cabin on the first day? Her name's Joy. We did some volunteer work in the local food pantry last night, then hung out at her apartment for a while."

"Carmen has a girlfriend," Marisol teased, unable to contain herself, but her mom wore a more puzzled expression.

"You snuck out to volunteer at a food pantry?" she asked. "Who *are* you and what have you done with my daughter?"

"I'm sorry," Carmen said, but Mom was laughing.

"Obviously, none of us begrudges you a little volunteer work," Dad said. "But if you're well enough to be running all over Emerald Hill, then you're well enough to follow my itinerary. No more crying wolf - you're spending the rest of the week with your family."

"I wasn't crying wolf," Carmen said. "But my ankle *does* feel better today, thanks for asking."

"Good," Dad said. "So tell me more about this breakfast place."

❄

THE CASTILLO CLAN went into Emerald Hill and ate at The Powder Hill Cafe, where Carmen had one of the best omelets of her life. Then because Mom and the twins had begun salivating the moment they drove through town and saw all the boutiques lining the main road, Dad found some room in the itinerary for a little bit of shopping.

"Are you healed enough to walk around a bit?" Mom asked Carmen.

"Yeah," she said. "My ankle's still a little stiff, but walking around will probably help loosen it up."

"There's my trooper," Dad said, patting Carmen on the back as they headed out of the café.

Their first stop was to a little dress shop right next to the café, where Mom bought the twins a pair of matching plaid dresses to wear on Christmas Day, and Carmen found a crushed velvet dress in a pretty maroon color. When Mom caught her running her hand down the soft fabric, she said, "We're going ice skating this afternoon.

You should get that – it would be perfect with a pair of skates and some fuzzy ear muffs."

Carmen laughed and pointed out the impracticality of wearing a dress that came down to mid-thigh in the middle of a Colorado winter, but her mom talked her into it.

"Come on," she said. "I can tell you like it. We'll call it a Christmas present."

Once they left the store, with Dad already starting to be weighed down by everyone's shopping bags, Carmen spotted a phone store on the other side of the street. She asked, "Could we go in there for a minute? I could get a replacement phone and stop hogging Mom's."

"It would be nice to get my phone back," Mom teased, so they went in and Carmen bought herself a new phone.

It took almost half an hour to get it set up, but that was pretty fast compared to New York standards. If she'd walked into an electronics store in the city without an appointment, she'd probably still be waiting for her new phone at closing time – especially with only five days until Christmas. Carmen was able to load a backed-up version of the phone she lost on the Outer Limits onto her new one, and by the time they walked out of the store, she was back to her old, hyper-connected self. There were a few dozen emails waiting for her, a few of them from work that she'd have to find a few minutes to answer, and her social media accounts had been blowing up without her checking on them compulsively. There were over a hundred notifications on Facebook alone, and a quick scroll through them told Carmen that the majority were humble brags from Cancun.

And there was the photograph that Joy had taken on the mountain. Carmen was smiling in it, her eyes pointing just a little bit higher than the camera lens, looking at Joy behind it. She'd done a pretty good job of making it look like a selfie, and the mountain really was impressive in the background. Carmen's finger hovered over it, about to share it for Brigid and Bentley to see, but then her Dad said, "Do we have everything we need here?"

"Yeah," Carmen answered, putting the phone in her pocket.

They went back outside and explored a couple more shops, and Carmen was surprised when Mom dragged them into a ski apparel shop.

"Are you serious?" Carmen asked as Mom made a bee line for a wall of women's ski jackets. "You're going to ski?"

Lucia Castillo had not willingly gone outside more than a handful of times in the last ten years, and even though Dad had tried to convince her to join the rest of the family when he penciled ski lessons into the itinerary, she'd given him a firm rejection. Now, though, with all eyes on her, she said, "Maybe."

"No way," Dad said, a smile forming. "Really?"

"I don't know," Mom said, getting a little irritated by the fuss they were making over her. She called a salesman over and pointed to one of the coats hanging on the wall, a silver and white one with a large, fur-lined hood. He retrieved the right size for her and she put it on, stepping in front of a large mirror to admire it. "I saw a woman at the dog sledding excursion who had a similar coat, and she looked so warm and fashionable."

"How much is it?" Dad asked, going over and reading the tag that hung from the sleeve. His eyes widened and he said, "Oh, Lucia. Really?"

She glanced at the tag, then said, "Well, it's a little more than I'd normally spend, but honey, it's so warm."

"Mom, when are you ever going to wear that again?" Carmen asked. It was a pretty coat, but her parents didn't normally make a fuss about money so whatever the price, it must have been extravagant.

"It gets cold in New York, too," Mom said, and asked the salesman to ring it up.

Dad said with a smirk, "You *better* come skiing with us now."

SIXTEEN

JOY

It was another long day at the lodge for Joy. Things had a way of getting more frantic the closer the holidays came, and Joy was having a hard time focusing on her work. She knew she should be thinking about the mentorship her boss offered her – it was a chance to advance her career after five years at the resort – but all she could think about was Carmen.

Carmen's soft skin. The way she tasted against Joy's lips. The sparkle in her eyes. The curves of her hips as she walked naked across Joy's apartment last night when they'd finished making love to get them each a glass of water from the kitchen. The way her voice never failed to send little tingles of pleasure into the back of Joy's head.

It had been so unexpected and so nice to look up from her work at the shelter last night and see Carmen standing in the doorway, and even nicer to bring her back to the apartment after. Joy spent most of the morning daydreaming about the next time they would meet, so when her phone started vibrating in her pocket, it felt like a fantasy to see Carmen's name on the screen.

"Hello?" Joy answered, ducking into an empty staff-only hallway to take the call.

"Hey, it's me," Carmen said, and a smile spread involuntarily over Joy's lips.

"I know," she said. Then she observed, "You got a new phone."

"Yeah," Carmen said. "We went into town this morning and had breakfast, then did a little shopping."

"Oh yeah?" Joy asked. "And what are you up to now? Still checking things off your dad's itinerary?"

"Yeah," Carmen said. "We just got to the resort's skating rink. My dad's waiting in line to rent us some skates right now. I was just wondering when your shift ends."

"Not for a while," Joy said with a sigh. "We're slammed with preparing for all the activities this week – the skating rink, sleigh rides, Santa's coming tomorrow for photographs, and of course all the last-minute check-ins. I might not be free until late this evening."

Joy's heart was aching to throw aside all of those obligations and just be with Carmen, but of course she couldn't do that, and she couldn't monopolize all of Carmen's time as much as she wanted to. She was here to spend Christmas with her family.

"Okay," Carmen said. "Well, I've got a phone now so just let me know when you're free and I'll see if I can slip away. I want to see you again."

The words ignited the desire in Joy's chest and rang

in her ears even after they hung up. She tried to go back to her work – she was in the middle of setting up the ballroom for a tea party that would take place that evening – but it only took a few minutes before curiosity got the best of her and she snuck away again. She was due for a break, anyway.

She grabbed her coat and went outside to the skating rink that had been set up at the far end of the ski area. It was pretty popular this morning, with about a hundred people skating in lazy circles on the ice, and it took Joy a couple of minutes before she spotted Carmen standing on the edge of the rink, watching her parents help her sisters get used to their skates on the far side of the rink. She wore a velvet dress beneath her plush coat, and a pair of fuzzy ear muffs that completed the look. Joy had to resist the urge to slide her arm around Carmen's waist as she went over and stood next to her.

"Hey," Carmen said, her eyes lighting up when she saw her. "What are you doing here?"

"Break time," Joy said, glancing at the rest of the Castillos. They were all a bit unsteady on the ice, and all completely absorbed in the task of not falling down, so she leaned in and gave Carmen a quick kiss. Then she asked, "You're not skating?"

"I thought about it," Carmen said. "But I didn't want to risk hurting my ankle again. I'm having fun watching my dad try desperately to stay on his feet, though. My sisters and mom are doing pretty well, though."

"Well, these are adorable in any case," Joy said, plucking at Carmen's ear muffs.

"I bought a few things this morning," she explained, pulling them off. They collapsed into a tight ball, and she folded and unfolded them a couple of times as she said, "We went into a vintage shop and I couldn't resist these because I used to have a pair just like them when I was a kid."

"I did, too," Joy said, then added with a laugh, "Only I hated mine. I was never the faux fur kind of girl. They look great on you, though."

She took them out of Carmen's hands and unfolded them, sliding them gently back over her ears. They watched Mr. and Mrs. Castillo and the twins making their way slowly around the perimeter of the skating rink for a few minutes. The girls caught on pretty quickly, gaining speed and leaving their parents behind, and when Carmen's parents finally made their way past the side of the rink that Carmen and Joy stood on, Mr. Castillo gave her an enthusiastic thumbs-up, then nearly lost his balance and had to cling to his wife to steady himself.

Carmen laughed, then she turned to Joy and said, "I had an idea."

"Oh yeah?"

"What does the homeless shelter normally do on Christmas Day?"

"Not a lot until evening," Joy said. "We don't have a huge budget so Tyler decided that it's best spent on making the dinner meal as nice as possible – every year there's ham and mashed potatoes, green bean casserole, and a few of the volunteers bring in pies for dessert. It's modest but nice. Why do you ask?"

"For Christmas, my parents usually give my sisters and I an allowance," Carmen said. "The twins love to shop so they're more than happy to buy their own presents, but I was thinking that I'd like to do something different with my Christmas money this year. I keep remembering all the expired stuff we had to throw away last night, and I haven't thought about my family using the food pantry when I was a kid in a long time. I'd like to help."

"You don't have to-" Joy objected, but Carmen didn't let her continue.

"I don't want to be another rich tourist who comes to Emerald Hill and takes from the mountain without giving back," she said. "I'd like to donate my Christmas money to the shelter, to be used however it'll be the most help."

"You should spend it on something you'll get to enjoy," Joy said.

"I'll enjoy helping the shelter more than owning yet another sweater, or whatever," Carmen insisted, slipping her hand into Joy's, and Joy thought that she might just lose it if this girl got any better. She was only here for a short time, and she was doing her darnedest to make Joy fall for her.

"Okay," Joy said. "If you're sure, then I know Tyler and all the visitors to the shelter will be very grateful."

"Can we go when you get done with work tonight?" Carmen asked.

"Sure," Joy said. "But I better get back to work now. I'll call you."

"Okay," Carmen said, and Joy squeezed her hand tighter for a moment, then let go. She had to get back into the ballroom to finish setting up tea cups on all the tables and making sure that everything was in place for the event, but her mind was only on Carmen.

SEVENTEEN
CARMEN

Carmen's mom eventually coaxed her onto the ice skating rink, looping her arm around Carmen's to hold her steady and protect her ankle from wobbling. She made a few turns around the rink, and when all their noses were red and their breath came out in dense clouds, they went back to the cabin. It had started to snow and they warmed up by the fire, sipping hot cocoa and watching the big white flakes come down outside.

It was about seven-thirty by the time Joy called to let Carmen know she'd finished all her responsibilities at the resort, and Carmen told her parents that she was going out for a couple of hours.

"Better not get attached," Mom warned, but Dad just nudged her with his elbow and smiled.

"Let her have a little Christmas romance," he said. "She's been working hard all year – she earned it."

"Don't stay out too late," Mom said, and then Joy's car pulled up in front of the cabin to pick Carmen up and she ran outside with a huge grin on her face. In the back of her mind she knew it was foolish to be so eager to see someone who would only be in her life for five more days, but she couldn't help the way her heart rose into her throat every time she saw Joy.

They drove into Emerald Hill and went to the shelter, where Tyler was busy getting cots and blankets out and setting them up in the shelter's great room for the people who would soon be coming in out of the cold and looking for a warm place to sleep. Joy brought him up to speed on Carmen's Christmas wish, and he asked, "Not to be blunt, but how much money are we talking about?"

"A thousand dollars," Carmen said. It felt strange and embarrassing to tell a stranger what her annual Christmas budget was, particularly with the shelter as the backdrop to this conversation, but he needed to know and she felt a little better knowing that the money would go to a worthy cause this year.

Tyler's eyes widened a little bit, although he struggled to keep his expression neutral, and Carmen pointedly avoided looking at Joy through this exchange. Their hands were linked, Joy's fingers warm in Carmen's, but she didn't want to look into Joy's eyes and see judgment or, worse, alienation.

Tyler said, "And what did you have in mind?"

"Whatever the shelter needs," Carmen said. "I was thinking it might be nice to do something special on Christmas Day, maybe give out blankets or warm clothing, but if you need the money for something else, please do what you think is best."

The three of them thought about it for a little while, and then Tyler said, "We should serve breakfast. We're never able to stretch the budget enough to do Christmas dinner and a hot morning meal, but I always feel bad sending them away hungry in the morning and telling them they have to wait til dinnertime."

"Great," Carmen said. "That sounds nice."

"That won't cost a thousand dollars, though," Tyler said. "More like a couple hundred."

"Then use the rest throughout the year," Carmen said. "Stock the food pantry when supplies are low."

He extended his hand to Carmen and she shook it, color rising into her cheeks, and she was happy when the moment had passed and she found herself alone outside with Joy. Her heart felt full and she was excited for the brighter holiday the shelter visitors would have now, but she was also eager to get the spotlight off of herself. She kissed Joy and then said, "What should we do now?"

"You don't need to go back to the cabin?" Joy asked, looking at Carmen with doe eyes that signaled desire. "Won't they miss you?"

"Maybe a little," Carmen said, wrinkling her nose as she smiled at Joy. "But I'd like to stay with you a bit longer. Can we go back to your apartment?"

"Of course," Joy said, taking her hand and pulling her eagerly toward her parked car.

❄

THIS TIME they made it all the way into Joy's bedroom.

They stripped each other naked, losing articles of clothing every step of the way down the short hallway, and collapsed into bed together, a tangle of limbs and desire. Joy's bed was soft and warm, the flannel sheets easy to sink into, and Carmen took her time exploring Joy's body this time.

She memorized the curve of her lips, the taste of peppermint on her skin, the softness of her curves and the muscles just beneath, earned from years on the slopes. She ran her fingers up and down over every inch of Joy's body, reading her and learning the different sounds of her pleasure as she kissed here, licked there, paused over her breasts and her thighs and her lips.

Carmen lay between Joy's thighs for almost half an hour, lazily tasting and touching her and teasing her closer and further from release. She wanted to enjoy this moment for as long as possible, freeze it in her mind and keep it there forever. If she only had five more days on the mountain, she'd make every moment that she had with Joy count.

DECEMBER 21

EIGHTEEN

CARMEN

Carmen jerked awake, squinting at the sun which was streaming through Joy's bedroom window and intensified by the reflection of the white snow outside. Joy was lying beside her, her smooth skin inviting Carmen to run her hand along it, and she realized that she'd nodded off last night with her arms around Joy.

"Shit," she said, sitting up. She'd only meant to close her eyes for a minute – her eyelids had been so heavy – and now it was morning. "Oh, shit."

"What's wrong?" Joy asked. She rolled over and rubbed the sleep from her eyes, revealing the perfect porcelain of her breasts, her nipples hard from the draft of the window. "Is it morning already?"

"Yeah," Carmen said, getting out of bed. Her panties and bra were on the floor near the bed, and the rest of her clothes were strewn throughout the apartment like breadcrumbs toward the door. "I didn't mean to fall asleep. My parents are probably wondering where the hell I am."

She hopped into her panties and Joy got out of bed, throwing on a robe and then going into the hallway to help Carmen gather up her clothes. When Joy put them all on the bed for her, Carmen went straight for her jacket, pulling her phone out of her pocket. There were three missed calls from Mom and one from Dad, and she realized with irritation that her phone had been set to silent the whole time so she never heard it ring.

Carmen called her mom's phone while she pulled her dress up over her hips and Joy went to her closet to get dressed.

"Oh good, you're not dead," Mom said with a sarcastic edge in her voice when she answered. "I was worried."

"I'm sorry," Carmen said. "I lost track of time and fell asleep."

"Fell asleep where?" her mom asked, and Carmen's neck went hot with embarrassment. She was twenty-two years old and yet sometimes she still felt like a teenager when it came to dealing with her parents.

"Umm," she stalled, trying to build up the courage to either tell the truth or lie. There was only one place she could be, though, and surely her mother knew that, so she just repeated, "I'm sorry, Mom. I'll be back soon."

They hung up and Carmen looked to Joy with a frown and said, "Well, that was embarrassing."

Joy went over and kissed Carmen's forehead. "Come on, I'll drop you off at the cabin. I've got to get to work soon anyway."

Then she produced the cheap ear muffs that Carmen

had been wearing yesterday, which had rolled almost into the kitchen last night in their haste to undress. She unfolded them and put them on Carmen's head.

They went out to Joy's car, shivering as they waited for the engine to warm up, and Joy asked, "So what's on the Castillo itinerary today?"

"I have no idea," she answered with a laugh. "I lost track somewhere around dog sledding. I think today's the day we finally hit the ski slopes? Or maybe that's supposed to be tomorrow and today is activities at the lodge."

"Santa's coming down from the North Pole for photographs today," Joy supplied. "I know your sisters said they're too old for Santa, but if the schedule allows, you should check it out. We turn the whole lobby into a winter wonderland and it's a lot of fun. You might even get to see me dressed like an elf if I can't sucker one of my subordinates into doing it."

"That I need to see," Carmen said, laughing.

Joy dropped her off in front of the cabin, then backtracked up the road to the lodge to begin her shift. When Carmen opened the door, the first thing she saw was her sisters sitting in the living room, sharing a breakfast of room service pancakes near the Christmas tree. The second thing she saw was her parents standing in the kitchen, her father's arms crossed over his chest.

"You slept over at that girl's apartment?" he asked, and Carmen immediately went red in the cheeks and neck. His tone wasn't exactly angry – mostly just disapproving – and that seemed to make it even worse. She was old enough now to make her own decisions, and she'd clearly made the wrong one by choosing Joy over her family.

"I didn't mean to," she explained. "I just fell asleep."

"We were worried," Mom said, her lips pursed and her voice low enough that the twins wouldn't catch the content of her words if they were listening. They were *definitely* listening, even if they were doing a pretty good job of pretending to be focused on their pancakes. "You could have at least called."

"Like I said, it was an accident," Carmen said. "I'm sorry that I worried you."

"Whatever happened to a family vacation?" Mom asked, and Carmen had to keep herself from snorting at this. It had been Mom who put up the biggest fight when Dad announced that they'd be coming to Emerald Mountain this year instead of Cancun, and now she was turning it back on Carmen. She said, "We've barely seen you since we arrived. You keep running off to be with some resort employee you just met."

"It's one thing to have a little fun with a fling on vacation," Dad said, keeping his voice low. "It's another to just not come home at night."

Carmen meant to say that she knew and she felt guilty for all the times she had chosen Joy over her family so far this week, but instead she said, "It's not a fling."

The words surprised even her, but she didn't like how flippant it had sounded when her dad used that word. No mere fling would consume so much of Carmen's mind, or fill her with a deep longing to be with Joy at every hour of the day. But could it really be any more than that with the knowledge that she'd be going back to New York the day after Christmas, half a country's distance away from here?

"Whatever it is, you need to be more responsible," Dad said. "We need to know where you are and you need to answer your phone. We were worried."

"I'm sorry," Carmen said.

Dad put his arm around her shoulder and accepted the apology, then offered to order her a stack of pancakes from room service. "They're lemon-ricotta and they're really good."

Carmen accepted this offer, and while she waited for her breakfast to be delivered, they went into the living room and sat down on the couch across from the twins. Carmen asked, "So what's on the itinerary today, Dad?"

"Your mom wanted to check out the resort spa," he said. "So she and the twins are going to go over the menu and book some services after breakfast. You could probably get a massage of some sort to help loosen things up if your ankle is still bothering you."

"It's basically back to normal, I think," Carmen said, putting her leg out in front of her and rolling her ankle back and forth a few times. It was pain-free and there was no more swelling, so her collision with Joy had been a fairly lucky hit and the sprain hadn't been bad. She asked, "Are you going to the spa?"

"I don't know," Dad said. "Mom wants me to get a pedicure but we're still in negotiations."

"I promise you'll like it," Mom said with a laugh.

Carmen thought about Joy's invitation to come to the winter wonderland in the lobby, and wondered if she could convince her sisters to give up their 'too old for Santa' insistence for a few minutes to check it out after their spa treatments.

"Then later we're all going into Denver for dinner," Dad added. "I made reservations at Mizuna because your mom's been dying to try the wild king salmon."

"They're known for it," Mom said. "Supposed to be out of this world."

"I don't care about the salmon," Maria said from her spot on the large ottoman. "I'm just waiting for tomorrow night."

"What's on the schedule for tomorrow night?" Carmen asked.

"We're having a chef come to the cabin, remember?" Mom said. "She was very highly recommended."

"Sounds good," Carmen said, and then she had an idea. "Hey, do you think I could invite Joy to join us if she's free?"

"Your girlfriend?" Maria asked in the same sing-song voice she'd used to tease Carmen the morning before when Joy's name had come up.

"Not exactly," Carmen said. She turned back to her parents to make her case. "Her roommate's out of town and her mom doesn't live in the area. I think she'd really like to share a family meal, especially with it getting so close to Christmas. Besides, this way you could get to know her and I can spend time with everyone. We all win."

She said this last bit with a wink, but it seemed to work – especially the part about Joy not having many people in her life right now. Carmen knew that would play on her mother's heartstrings, and in the end, it worked.

"Bring her," Mom said. "I'm sure Chef Julia won't mind one more guest – I'll just let her know."

"Thanks, Mom," Carmen said, giving her a quick hug just as there was a knock on the door and her breakfast arrived.

❄

CARMEN DIDN'T GET a chance to see Joy again after their frantic morning together – Dad kept her busy with spa treatments and despite Joy's lamentation she didn't have to dress as an elf for Santa's visit to the lobby, which Carmen succeeded in dragging her sisters to. They said they were too old and that the wonderland of cotton batting and glittery fake snow was 'little kid stuff,' but after a few minutes they lost themselves in the moment and Mom had a good time taking pictures of them exploring the life-sized gingerbread house, plucking candy canes off the enormous Christmas tree, and even waiting in line to see Santa Claus.

In the evening they went into Denver for their dinner reservations, the hour-long limo ride both ways eating into Carmen's free time, and by the time they got back to the cabin it was late and she was tired. She texted Joy a few times throughout the day, checking in with her, and just as she was crawling into bed that night, she called to invite Joy to dinner the next night.

"I don't know," Joy hedged, and Carmen was surprised that she objected.

"Do you have plans?" Carmen asked. "I'm sorry, I shouldn't have assumed you would be free."

"It's not that," Joy said. "I've just never done the whole 'meet the parents' thing before, and with your family in particular, I might be too intimidated to be any fun."

"Intimidated?" Carmen asked, surprised. "I know you only know them as resort visitors, but there's nothing to be intimidated by."

"Really?" Joy asked with a snort. "You're staying in one of the nicest accommodations the resort has to offer. The money you donated to Tyler will feed and shelter people for at least a couple of weeks and to you it amounts to nothing more than a stocking stuffer. Your family might have started out from humble beginnings, but your world is *so* different from mine. Yes, it's intimidating."

Carmen felt embarrassed like she always did when people looked at her and saw her wealth. She'd foolishly hoped that Joy was able to look beyond it – Carmen thought that after working at the resort for so long and being surrounded by affluent travelers she might be desensitized to it, and she didn't like knowing that Joy saw that part of her after all. Her bank account, the lifestyle that her parents had thrust upon her, was only one aspect of her life and she didn't want that to be the thing that Joy focused on.

There was one thing that might help, though.

"I haven't told you what my dad did to make his money," she said. "You don't have to come to dinner if you don't want to, but I have a feeling you'll think differently about us after I tell you. Do you want to know?"

"Very badly," Joy said with a laugh. "I'd be lying if I said I wasn't curious."

"Most people are," Carmen said. "You're going to laugh."

"I'm ready."

"Have you heard of the app GoGet?" she asked.

"That's the one where you can get people to run your errands for you, right?" Joy asked.

"Yeah," Carmen said. "It's like Uber, only instead of getting a ride, you hire someone to go out and get whatever you need and bring it to you."

"Are you telling me your dad invented GoGet?" Joy asked.

"Yeah," Carmen said. "He came up with the idea, hired some people to program the app, and it turned out to be his million-dollar idea. I've been working on developing a drone division since I graduated from college, so with any luck it'll become a multimillion-dollar company within the next few years."

"Wow," Joy said. "And this is supposed to help me stop being intimidated how?"

"I'm about to tell you its origin story," Carmen said. "Very few people know this, and I have to swear you to secrecy that you won't share this information. My dad's kind of embarrassed about how GoGet was born."

"Okay, you've piqued my interest," Joy said. "I won't tell a soul."

"It definitely didn't start out as an app," Carmen said. "My dad was always inventing things when I was a kid – he'd come home almost weekly with a new idea, so excited and so sure that it was going to be brilliant. They rarely were, and my mom started to get kind of irritated with him after a while. I think there are only so many times you can be a cheerleader for an idea that gets abandoned a week later when a new one takes over.

"GoGet was one of his earliest ideas, from his twenties. He called it Beer Run back then, and the original idea was that he could call a friend who owed him a favor whenever the Massachusetts winters were too bitter or he was just too tired from a long day at work, and that friend had to go on a beer run or a whatever run and bring it over to the house for him. It was a clever way of exploiting his friends, but it wasn't really an invention until apps came into wide use and the world was finally ready for Beer Run to turn into GoGet.

"By that time my dad had been laid off from his job at the factory, and my mom had reached the height of her annoyance at his inventions. She wanted him to quit wasting his time on them and focus on providing for his family, so he did. He buckled down, started looking at job boards and putting out resumes. He set his inventions aside, and other than GoGet, he hasn't really picked the hobby back up again since.

"So his efforts paid off and he got a call about a job not too long after he was laid off, but on the morning of the interview, he realized that his only pair of dress shoes were horribly scuffed and he was badly in need of shoe polish. He had to watch me while Mom was at work and he had no time to go to the store, so he decided to call in a favor and have one of his friends go on a run for shoe polish. It wasn't until Dad was halfway through the job interview that the gears really started turning on the possibilities of using technology to bring Beer Run to the masses. He immediately started calling around to see who could program it for him, and it was midnight before he remembered to tell Mom that he'd gotten the job he applied for."

Joy laughed and said, "So your family fortune comes from your dad being too lazy to get his own beer when he was in his twenties. That's great."

"And now you know why you shouldn't be intimidated by any of us," Carmen said. "So will you come to dinner?"

"Yeah," Joy said. "I'd love to."

"Just don't tell my dad that I told you that story," Carmen cautioned.

"Sure," Joy agreed. "It's kind of sad that he doesn't invent anymore, though. It sounds like he really had a zest for it."

"Yeah, he did," Carmen said. "I think he's just too busy these days. It's a surprising amount of work being an app mogul."

DECEMBER 22

NINETEEN

JOY

Joy went to the Castillo cabin the next evening, still feeling a little bit anxious. She'd never met a love interest's family before – most of her relationships never got that serious – and she knew that by the end of the week, she'd probably never see this family again. Despite that knowledge, she couldn't shake the idea that tonight was a big deal and she wanted to do her best to impress Carmen's family. When she knocked on the door, Carmen answered and gave her a quick kiss.

"Thanks for coming," she said, looking Joy up and down and smiling in approval of the dress pants and neatly pressed plaid shirt that Joy had agonized over. She hadn't known whether this was too formal, not formal enough, or just right, but in the end, plaid always put her into a festive spirit and her choice was validated when Carmen leaned in and whispered in Joy's ear, "You look hot."

"So do you," Joy said. "As always."

Carmen was wearing a short black dress with three-quarter length sleeves that made her look sexy and elegant all at once. She had on a modest string of pearls and she was wearing her long, raven-colored hair up in a bun, a few curled tendrils framing her face. As she led Joy into the cabin to meet the rest of the family, she pointed to a small gift bag that Joy had looped over her arm and asked, "What's that?"

"You'll see," Joy said with a smile, and then Carmen introduced her to the rest of her family.

They were all standing around the kitchen island, chatting with their other guest for the evening, the chef, while she cut vegetables and talked them through the dish she was preparing.

"Joy's here," Carmen announced and they all turned to acknowledge her.

"Umm, hi," she said, her nerves getting the better of her once again. "Nice to meet you... again."

"Come on in and make yourself at home," Mr. Castillo said, smiling gregariously at her. Then he chuckled and added, "Although I guess this place is more your home than ours. *We're* the guests here, it's your resort."

"It's not *my* resort, Mr. Castillo," Joy said. "I just work here."

"Please, call me Tony," he said, extending his hand and catching hers in a firm handshake. Then he made introductions all the way around the island. "That's my wife, Lucia, and my daughters Marisol and Maria, and Chef Julia who will be preparing our meal tonight."

"We've met," Joy said, nodding at Julia. "She has catered some wonderful meals for events taking place at the resort. Thank you for having me to dinner."

"Our pleasure," Lucia said. "Do you want something to drink? We've got red wine, juice, soda, water, or I could call for room service if none of those things suits you."

"A glass of wine would be great," Joy said, feeling flustered at the abundance of options being laid out before her. She wondered if the menu would show the same lack of restraint, and if the Castillos were used to having everything their hearts desired.

"I'm just about to put the entre in the oven," Julia said, then she added for Joy's benefit, "You'll be having beef wellington with sautéed new potatoes and green beans. It'll be ready in about thirty minutes if everyone would like to have a seat in the living room until then."

"Sure, we'll get out of your hair," Tony said with a wink, leading everyone over to the living room. "I'm sure we can find a way to entertain ourselves until then."

"Oh," Joy said, remembering the gift bag on her arm. "I think I've got something."

"Oh yeah?" he asked. Carmen was looking at her with curiosity, eager to find out what she had up her sleeve, and Joy was pretty sure she was going to love it.

"I brought a little before-dinner treat for the girls to try," she said, sliding the bag off her arm and looking at Carmen as she produced a jar of molasses. "Do you want to try making snow candy?"

"No way," Tony said as soon as he saw it. "Carmen,

you remember when you were a kid and we tried that? Man, what a disaster!"

"Yeah," Carmen said, grinning at Joy. "I sure do. Girls, come over here."

She called her sisters over and they looked at the molasses skeptically. Joy wondered for a moment if she should have brought a more traditional gift – a bottle of wine, or maybe a pack of holiday crackers for the twins to play with – but she was committed now so she explained to the girls, "Carmen told me the other day that when she was a kid, she read that you could pour molasses on the snow and it would turn into candy. She tried it and it was a big mess, but I wanted to see if we can try it again and get better results. I looked it up and apparently, there's a little more to it than just pouring molasses on snow."

She shot a comical look at Carmen, then pulled a small box of brown sugar out of the gift bag.

"If Chef Julia doesn't mind the intrusion, we can boil the molasses along with some sugar," she said, "and make candy the way that Laura Ingalls Wilder intended. What do you guys think?"

"I'll give it a whirl," Marisol said with a shrug. She didn't look overly enthusiastic about it, but at least she'd agreed to try. The elder Castillos, on the other hand, looked downright excited – Tony was smiling approvingly and Lucia looked curious. And the look on Carmen's face... that look warmed Joy's belly.

Joy looked to Julia in the kitchen and she said, "The more the merrier. I'll make room for you."

"Alright, let's do this," Carmen said, and she put her

hand on Joy's back as they all headed over to the kitchen island. It brought color to Joy's cheeks, and somehow melted the remaining apprehension that she felt. Everything was right now, and she immersed herself in the process of making molasses into snow candy.

"Okay, first we need to gather up some snow," Joy said.

Julia dug around in the storage beneath the island, pulling out a couple of cookie sheets and asking, "Will these work?"

"Perfect," Joy said, giving one each to Maria and Marisol. "Can you two go outside and collect some snow? Pack it firmly and make sure it's clean."

Tony accompanied the girls out the back door, past the snow-covered patio and into the yard beyond. Joy knew there was at least a half-foot of untouched snow out there, and they'd have no trouble filling their cookie sheets.

While the girls gathered snow, Joy worked on boiling the molasses while Carmen and Lucia watched. She poured the jar into a saucepan, along with half a cup of brown sugar, then stirred it constantly as she waited for it to boil.

"Ah," Carmen said with a smile. "That would be where I went wrong as a kid."

"I remember daddy being so mad about that," Lucia said. "I came home from work and there was molasses all over the yard."

"I seem to remember a different person getting angry," Carmen said, laughing and teasing her mother.

Joy smiled at them, suddenly missing her own mother. They used to have moments like this when she was a kid, picking on each other for the sake of it, before her mom's rheumatism got so bad she lost her sense of humor.

Joy was thinking that she ought to call her again after dinner, and again it occurred to her that Danny and her mom were right about leaving Emerald Hill. Then Carmen nudged Joy's shoulder with her own and said, "It's boiling."

"Oh," Joy said, stirring it down and removing it from the heat. Then the twins and Tony came back inside and Lucia went over to help them carry the sheets of snow without spilling it all across the cabin.

"Thanks for doing this," Carmen said, giving Joy a quick peck on the cheek. "This is really sweet."

"Don't thank me yet," Joy said with a laugh. "All I did was research it – I have no idea how it'll taste."

Julia passed Joy a measuring cup to pour the molasses mixture into after it had cooled down a little bit. She filled the cup and then set it on the kitchen island next to the two baking sheets of snow Marisol and Maria had collected.

"Be careful, it's hot," she said. "What you want to do is slowly drizzle the liquid on top of the snow. Try to keep it thin, sort of like you're making a funnel cake, so the snow can freeze the molasses."

The whole family stood around the island watching as the two youngest Castillos took turns drizzling the mixture onto the snow, and when the pans were full of stringy lines of hardened molasses, everyone took a piece out of the snow.

"Moment of truth," Joy said, smiling at the twins.

"It's already much more successful than what I ended up with as a kid," Carmen said, snapping off a little piece between her teeth.

Joy tasted her own piece, watching as the Castillos each reacted to the candy. The twins both made disgusted faces, Lucia put her piece down pretty quickly, and Carmen looked more than a little disappointed. As for Joy, she found it to be a little bitter, very rich, and somewhat akin to taking the essence of a gingerbread house and concentrating it into a frozen piece of syrup.

"What do you think?" she asked everyone.

"Gross," the twins said in unison. Then Maria asked, "Is dinner almost ready?"

"Just a few more minutes," Julia said, tasting her own piece of snow candy. She shrugged and said, "It's not bad. If you don't like the taste of molasses then it's not going to do much for you, of course."

Carmen smiled at Joy and said, "I don't think they could ever live up to the idea of them that I got from reading *Little House on the Prairie*, but they're a thousand times better than my first attempt."

"It was a fun activity," Lucia said. She laughed and added, "I think the twins enjoyed it until the tasting part."

Tony was the only one who unabashedly enjoyed them, reaching for another piece in the snow and saying, "I think they're good."

JOY

❄

JULIA'S BEEF wellington was ready shortly after, just in time for the Castillos to get the bitter taste of molasses off their tongues. Everyone sat down around the large dining table beside the kitchen and Joy slid into the seat next to Carmen. She put her hand beneath the tablecloth, lacing her fingers into Carmen's and resting her hand on top of Carmen's thigh.

"It's going well, right?" she asked. The snow candy had not won anyone other than Tony over, but they'd all had fun making it, and they seemed to be getting along.

Carmen squeezed Joy's hand and smiled at her. Julia was bringing plates to the table, setting them down in front of Tony and Lucia first, and while they were occupied with admiring their meals, she leaned in and said into Joy's ear, "You're fantastic and everyone loves you. They'd be crazy not to."

It sent a rush of adrenaline through Joy's system, and just as her own plate was set down in front of her, she wondered if there was any subconscious significance to Carmen's choice of words. *Everyone* loved her? She brought Carmen's hand to her lips, kissing her fingers quickly before letting her go so they could enjoy their meal.

She'd eaten Julia's food before so she knew that it would be good, but it turned out to be more extravagant and delicious than she could have imagined. Her mouth was watering before she'd even picked up her silverware, and the whole cabin smelled like home-cooked comfort food. They all complimented Julia on a job well done, and then settled in to eat.

They all seemed to break off into their own conversations – the twins were talking about the things they knew were waiting under the tree for them and that they were eager to open nonetheless, while Tony and Lucia reminisced about their house in Massachusetts and how their version of Christmas back then was wildly different from the one they were enjoying now.

"Oh," Joy said to Carmen after a minute of getting accustomed to this sort of disjointed style of dinner conversation, "I wanted to tell you that Tyler cashed the check you wrote him today, in case you need to know to balance your books or something."

"Good," Carmen said. "Is he going to be able to get everything he needs for the Christmas morning breakfast?"

"I'm sure he will," Joy said. "He's got plenty of money thanks to you. I think what he needs most is more hands on deck to help out."

Overhearing the subject of their conversation, Lucia cut in to say, "Carmen told us a bit about your work at the homeless shelter in town, Joy. How did you get involved with it?"

"I went there as part of a volunteering day with my high school class," she explained. "I saw the difference that I could make in my community, so I just kept going back to help."

"What is it that you do there?" Tony asked.

"Just about anything that the shelter coordinator asks

me to do," Joy said, "which is pretty similar to my job at the resort. My biggest project every year is organizing the food pantry, which tends to get pretty out of control around the holidays. Carmen can attest to that – she helped me with it a couple of days ago."

"It really does need some intervention," Carmen said with a laugh. "But we got it sorted out, at least for a while."

"Interesting," Tony said. "What exactly is the problem with the organization system?"

"It's perfect for about ten months out of the year," Joy said. "It's just that with the amount of donations we receive every year during the holiday season, it's impossible to keep the freshest foods at the back and everything shelved according to type. It all ends up disorganized and I think we waste more food than we would if we had a better system."

"Hmm," Tony said, sitting back in his chair and setting down his fork as soon as he'd polished off his beef wellington. He rubbed his hand over his chin and said, "I wonder if we couldn't figure out a solution to your problem."

Joy shot a look at Carmen. She wanted to inquire about his inventions, to ask what he meant by that, but she wasn't sure if she could do that without giving away the fact that Carmen had told her about the origins of GoGet. Instead, she glanced at Carmen and then said, "Did you know that your daughter made a very generous donation to the shelter the other day? We're going to be able to serve Christmas breakfast to nearly two hundred people who might not have had more than one meal on that day, and restock the pantry after the holiday rush is over."

"Is that so?" Lucia asked, smiling at Carmen. "That's sweet of you."

"I was thinking about when I was a kid," Carmen explained. "You took me with you a couple of times when we had to use a food pantry, and there wasn't a lot to choose from. I wanted to help."

"That's great, kiddo," Tony said, but he still seemed preoccupied, and Joy guessed that he was thinking about her pantry organization problem.

After dinner, while they waited for Julia's award-winning chocolate soufflés to be ready, they all went into the living room and sat down on the couches. Joy and the rest of the adults drank coffee, while Marisol and Maria had hot cocoa, and after a while Lucia gestured at the Christmas tree in front of the window, saying to Joy, "I've been wondering this since we arrived. Does every cabin have the same tree in it?"

"No," Joy said. "Every cabin has its own theme and they're each decorated differently. Your theme is 'rustic Christmas,' see? Your tree has a burlap garland, some wood slice ornaments, and your mantle is decorated to match. Last year I actually spent an entire day trimming every single one of the trees in the twenty cabins, plus the big one in the resort lobby. This year I got to pass the task off to another coworker, and you know what? I actually missed it – that job always puts me in the mood for the holidays."

"We haven't trimmed a tree in at least five years," Lucia observed. "I didn't even really miss it until now. Tony, when do you think was the last time we had a tree?"

"I think you're right," he said. "The twins were just starting kindergarten and we went to a tree farm upstate. We got that tall one you loved that I practically had to climb in order to decorate the tall branches."

"It was so pretty, though," Lucia said. "And the fresh pine smell was so festive."

"What happened after that?" Joy asked. "Why don't you get trees anymore?"

"I don't think they have pine trees in Cancun," Lucia said with a laugh. "I think that was the last year we stayed at home for Christmas, and after that we were content to look at palm trees."

DECEMBER 23

TWENTY

JOY

Joy stayed at the Castillo cabin for a while that night, enjoying every bite of the incredibly rich soufflé that Julia baked for them and then stuck around to talk with Carmen and her parents after the twins headed into their bedroom to play with their tablets. Lucia and Tony were much easier to talk to than Joy had feared, and when she found out that they'd been putting off skiing lessons for fear of the crowded slopes, she offered to take them out the next day.

"Are you sure?" Lucia asked.

"Absolutely," Joy said. "I've been skiing and snowboarding since I could walk. I'd be happy to teach you and save you the price of a private lesson. You can't leave Emerald Hill without conquering the mountain."

So she got up early on her day off and met the Castillo clan in the rental area of the ski lodge. Lucia was all too happy to have a place to wear her expensive ski jacket and prove her family wrong about its usefulness, and the twins were excited to try their hand at a pair of snowblades when Joy explained to them that they were a little more manageable than regular skis, and infinitely more cool. Tony was the only hold-out, absolutely convinced that he was going to fall down and break both of his legs if he went out on the slopes.

"I promise I won't let anything happen to you," Joy said as she tried to tempt him to get into the ski rental line.

"Did you make that promise to my daughter before she twisted her ankle?" Tony asked stubbornly.

"No," Joy said with a laugh. "She didn't get hurt learning to ski – she got hurt standing around where other people were skiing."

Carmen rolled her eyes good-naturedly and tugged on her dad's jacket to get him into the line, but the patriarch of the Castillo family would not be budged. He said, "I just know I'm going to break something out there. I'll watch you guys from the lodge and have some hot cocoa waiting when you need to warm up."

Lucia shook her head at him and said, "I can't believe you're chickening out on one of your own itinerary items."

Then he headed upstairs to the lodge and Joy got everyone else the equipment they needed. Joy rented a pair of skis for herself as well since she hadn't had the time to have her snowboard binding replaced, and of course it would be easier for her to teach the Castillos to ski if she had matching equipment.

Carmen started to get a little anxious as they lugged

their equipment over to the benches to button up their jackets and put on their boots. She said, "I don't know, maybe I should sit this one out with Dad."

"Is your ankle feeling okay?" Lucia asked as she helped the twins put on their boots.

"It's fine," Carmen said. "But I don't want to twist it all over again."

"You won't," Joy said.

"How can you be sure?" Carmen challenged.

"Well, for one thing you'll be wearing the proper equipment," Joy said. "Those boots are stiff for a reason – they'll protect your ankles. And for another thing, I'm going to give you lessons so that you'll be safe out there."

Carmen still looked a little concerned, but Joy convinced her it would be fine.

"Sheesh," she said as she shoved her foot into her boot. "I'm surprised you guys settled on a ski vacation if you're all so afraid of the slopes."

"I think it was more about the white Christmas and the snowy atmosphere," Lucia said with a laugh.

"Well, Emerald Mountain has plenty of that," Joy said. "But you're going to learn to ski while you're here – I'm making it my mission."

The five of them finished getting their gear on and zipping up their coats, and then Joy helped them all make their way outside. She showed them how to walk in the stiff ski boots – heel to toe, heel to toe, creating a rhythm as they walked.

"You have to kind of rock in them," Joy said, demonstrating for her audience. "Get some momentum going."

"Like this?" Carmen asked, trying to do the same. She was clumsy, but she got it after a minute and they all came to a stop at the base of a very gentle hill so that Joy could show them how to step into their skis.

Joy bent down to help the twins into their snowblades, letting them put their hands on her shoulders to steady themselves as they snapped their boots into the bindings. Then once everyone got used to their skis, Joy taught them the basics – the back and forth motion of the skis that could be exaggerated to slow down or curtailed to speed up, the use of the poles for balance, and most importantly, how to point the tips of their skis into a triangle shape, or snow plough, to stop.

Then she pointed up at the novice hill directly in front of the lodge and said, "You ready to try it out?"

"Yes," the twins said, while in the exact same moment, Carmen and her mother said, "No."

Joy laughed, and then reminded them, "You said you wanted to learn how to ski. It's not that bad – this is barely a hill."

"Tell that to the medics when they have to come help me off it," Carmen said with a laugh.

"Oh, please," Joy said. "This slope is so tiny we wouldn't even bother calling the medics – we'd just shove you down to the bottom with our ski poles."

That got a laugh from the twins and helped to break the tension. Joy showed them how to build some momentum with their skis across the flat ground at the base of the hill, then led them all over to a tow rope, which was nothing more than a rope leading up the side of the hill with a series of plastic handles that came by every ten feet and carried skiers to the top of the novice slope.

"There's no chair lift?" Carmen asked, and Joy laughed.

"Not for a hill this size," she said. "The tow rope isn't difficult – you're just going to position yourself beside the rope and watch behind you for a handle. When it comes by, grab on and hold tight until you get to the top of the hill."

"Yeah, right," Carmen scoffed. "What if I trip?"

"Then you let go of the rope and get out of the way before the next person on the rope runs you over," Joy said. "You'll get the hang of it, but you have to practice."

Carmen went first, approaching the rope with a little more cajoling from Joy and letting several handles pass her by before she finally got up the courage to grab one of them. It jolted her forward and Joy called to her, "Keep your skis parallel until you get to the top."

Joy watched with a little bit of apprehension until Carmen was about halfway up the hill without incident, then she got Marisol in position next. Both of the twins were much braver – fearlessness was a trait of the young – and they grabbed the tow rope without incident. Joy watched when Carmen got to the top of the hill, wincing as she accidentally crossed her skis over each other and nearly fell, but she got it sorted out and used her poles to keep herself upright. Then Joy got Lucia on the rope and then hopped on herself.

When the entire Castillo family had arrived on the

flat area at the top of the hill, their skis pointed down toward the lodge, Joy showed them how to dig their poles deep into the snow to keep from sliding down the hill. Then she asked, "Are you guys ready?"

"Yeah," Marisol said, looking like she was ready to push off and go flying down the hill. Maria looked a little more cautious, Carmen looked worried, and Lucia looked just about ready to take off her skis and walk back down the hill.

"You're all going to do just fine," Joy reassured them. "Just give each other plenty of space and if you feel like you're losing control, just sit down in the snow and you'll stop. Oh, and have fun – you're on vacation, so stop looking at me like I'm sending you to your death."

The twins went down first. Marisol shot down the hill so fast that Joy started getting nervous, shouting with her hands cupped around her mouth for the girl to snow plough when she got to the bottom, otherwise she'd end up smacking straight into the lodge. She didn't manage to get her skis into that triangle formation Joy had showed her, but she did have the good sense to sit down when she got to the flat part of the hill to keep from crashing into people traveling back and forth from the lodge to the rest of the hills.

Maria and Lucia took a more conservative route, ploughing almost all the way down the hill and making their way slowly and cautiously to the bottom.

Then it was Carmen's turn. Joy watched from the top of the hill as she started out in plough like the rest of her family, and then about halfway down the hill she got brave and leveled her skis out for a few seconds, picking up speed and wobbling a bit but keeping her footing. Joy cheered her on until she returned to the safety of plough, and then Joy made her way down the hill, swaying back and forth across it to get the most out of the little slope.

"What did you guys think?" she asked when she reached the bottom, and the reviews were mixed. The twins had loved it, Carmen thought it was fine, and Lucia was still pretty sure she might die.

They all took a few more stabs at the bunny hill, and Joy watched as they got a little more comfortable with the tow rope and with their skis with each successive run. They spent a couple of hours on the slopes, and even though they never got up the courage to try any but the smallest hills, they all had a good time.

Even Lucia loosened up after a few more uneventful runs, although it didn't take long for her to heat up in her expensive coat. On their fifth or sixth time down the hill, they met at the top and she said, "I think this is my last run. Who knew it would be possible to sweat on the side of a mountain?"

"I could have told you that," Joy said. "Although that coat you're wearing would be great if you ever got caught in an avalanche."

Carmen laughed, and Lucia added, "I think I'm going to head over to the lodge and see what Daddy's up to after this run. Anyone want to come inside and warm up with me for a little while?"

The twins agreed, especially after their mom made mention of ordering some manner of sugary *après ski* snack, and the three of them made their last run down the slopes, leaving Joy and Carmen at the top of the hill. Carmen was just about to shove off when Joy reached out and grabbed her by the hem of her coat.

"Hey, hold back a minute."

"What's wrong?" Carmen asked, and Joy pulled her backward until their skis entwined.

"Nothing," she said, wrapping her arms around Carmen's waist and turning her head to kiss her. "I just wanted to tell you I'm having a really good time with you this week."

"I am, too," Carmen said, then after a brief pause she added, "It's a shame the week is almost over."

"Let's not think about that right now," Joy said. It sent physical pain into her chest to think about the fact that they had a mere three days left together. She held Carmen tight and kissed her like it was her last opportunity, and then Carmen reached into her coat pocket and pulled out her phone.

She opened the camera app and held the phone out in front of her, saying, "I want a souvenir to remember you by."

Joy squeezed her tighter and hated the idea, but she kissed Carmen's cheek as she snapped the photo. Then while she was tucking the phone back in her pocket, Joy asked, "Are you going to send that to your friends in Cancun?"

"No," Carmen said. "This one's just for me."

TWENTY-ONE

CARMEN

It began to snow and Carmen and Joy came in from the cold soon after her mother and sisters went to meet Dad in the lodge. Instead of following them, Carmen grabbed Joy by the collar of her ski jacket after they'd returned their rental skis and pulled her into a deep kiss.

"Do you want to go back to the cabin?" she asked. "I'm sure my family will be in the lodge drinking hot cocoa and basking in the fact that they can now call themselves skiers for at least another hour."

"So you're saying there's a good chance we could have the cabin to ourselves for a little while," Joy said.

"Yes," Carmen answered, giving Joy a seductive smile. "That is exactly what I'm saying."

"Sounds nice," Joy answered. "Should we go make sure your mom stays occupied in the lounge first?"

"Nah," Carmen said. "Better to let them assume we're still on the slopes."

Joy laughed, then let Carmen drag her out the door. The snow was falling fast now and the plows hadn't gotten back on the roads just yet, so the walk to the cabin felt longer than it really was. They walked hand in hand the whole way there, Carmen resenting the fact that it was cold and that meant there were two layers of gloves between their fingers. She spent the walk telling Joy just how sexy she'd looked skiing down the bunny slopes, and how she couldn't tear her eyes away from her the whole time they were out there.

As soon as they got inside the empty cabin, Carmen pushed Joy up against the front door and unzipped her coat, putting her arms around Joy's waist and holding her close. Joy let out a little moan of pleasure, and then as Carmen slipped her hands beneath Joy's sweater, her moan turned into a gasp and she said, "Ooh, your hands are like icicles."

"Sorry," Carmen said, rubbing them together and smiling at Joy while she tried to get the blood flowing again. She wasn't used to the challenges of cold weather seduction, and this little delay only served to amp up her desire for Joy all the more.

"It's okay," Joy said, taking both of Carmen's hands in hers. She put her lips to Carmen's fingertips and exhaled hot breath on them. Looking up at Carmen, she murmured against her skin, "I've got ways to warm you up."

The purring quality of her voice sent a shiver through Carmen, and her pulse quickened as she waited to find out what Joy had in mind. Joy unzipped Carmen's coat, pushing it down her shoulders and hanging it on the coat rack near the door, and then she shimmied out of hers as well. She kissed her, tongue sliding over her lips, and they kicked off their boots without allowing themselves to separate from each other.

"Come on," Joy growled, her voice vibrating against Carmen's skin as she walked her backward toward the hallway.

"My room?" Carmen asked.

"No," Joy said. "I told you I'd warm you up, and while I'd love nothing more than to lay you down in front of the fireplace and kiss every inch of your body, I think I'd be ruining your parents' high opinion of me if they found us in that position."

"So what do you have in mind?" Carmen asked as Joy slowly backed her down the hall, her hands exploring her as they went.

"There's more than one way to warm up after a day on the slopes," Joy said, and she pulled Carmen into the bathroom. Closing the door, she pushed Carmen against it and their bodies came together firmly as they kissed again. Then she said, "Don't move."

Carmen let out a little whimper as Joy stepped away from her, giving her a wink that did more to melt her insides than any fireplace could. She was obedient, though, keeping her back against the door as she watched Joy go over to the large bathtub in front of the window. It looked out on the same secluded part of the mountain as the living room, nothing but snow-covered trees and steep mountain peaks behind them, but the world outside of the cabin could have burned and been reduced to ash for all she knew, because she couldn't see anything beyond Joy.

Joy bent and turned on the faucet, testing the water with her hand and then, while the tub filled, she poured in a little bit of soap from a bottle on the lip of the tub. Then she turned around and walked slowly, teasingly, back to Carmen, her hips swaying with every step.

"Do you want to share a bubble bath with me?" she asked when she joined her again, her hand going to the front of Carmen's sweater and their hips connecting. Carmen's heart was pounding and she would have agreed to anything if it meant getting closer to Joy.

"I would love to," Carmen said, and Joy took her hands, twining their fingers together and pinning them on either side of Carmen's head.

Then she bent down and gently kissed the exposed skin at the crook of her neck. She pulled Carmen's sweater over her head, dropping it to the floor, and Carmen felt her skin beginning to prickle with goosebumps. The tub behind them was filling with warm water and beginning to fill the room with steam, but she still wanted Joy's warmth most of all.

She'd had enough teasing, being pinned to the door and her hands kept from Joy's body. She pushed off the door and put her hands on Joy's waist, guiding her over to the sink, where she lifted Joy onto the counter and their hips connected once again in the most tantalizing, tormenting way.

TWENTY-TWO

JOY

What started off slow and teasing quickly turned into a frenzy as Carmen put her hands on Joy. The touch ignited her whole body, and everywhere Carmen's fingers brushed over her it felt like a thousand little sparks going off and spreading deeper into her core. Joy leaned in to kiss her as they finished undressing each other, shedding layer after layer that had been so necessary on the slopes but which were only keeping them from each other now.

The bathtub was close to full and Carmen's skin was dimpled with goosebumps despite the steam that fogged the mirrors. The marble countertop of the sink was cold against Joy's hips and she slid off it, guiding Carmen backward to the tub beneath the window. She turned off the faucet, then led Carmen to the edge of the tub. It was sunken into the floor, large enough for two to share it comfortably, and Joy held Carmen's hand as they stepped slowly into the warm water, getting used to the temperature as they sank into the tub.

When they were sitting down, the water just below Carmen's breasts and the bubbles teasingly obscuring her nakedness, Carmen leaned back against the edge of the tub. A few tendrils of her hair floated along the surface of the water and her skin was dewy with steam. Joy crawled over to her on her knees, slowly so as to keep the water from sloshing over the edge of the tub. Beneath the surface, she put her hands on Carmen's thighs and separated them slowly. Carmen let out a little whimper and sank further into the water as Joy's stomach and then her pubic bone slid between her thighs.

Joy could feel Carmen's body tense up, seeking her, and she moved her palm between Carmen's legs. Joy kissed her – first her lips, and then her jaw, and then her collar bone, and then as Carmen arched her back at Joy's underwater touch, her breasts rose above the surface and Joy licked the little droplets of moisture from her skin.

Carmen put her hands on Joy, her palms gliding over her breasts and then down her sides to squeeze and caress every curve. Joy closed her eyes, taking in every unique sensation of this moment – the water that moistened her lips every time she kissed Carmen's breasts and her neck. The sweet cocoa butter smell of the bubble bath. The warmth of the water mixing with the warmth of Carmen's hands on her. The uncertainty of where she ended and Carmen began.

She was inside her and against her, their movements creating waves out of the water. Carmen put her head back against the porcelain edge of the tub and let out a long, low moan into the steamy room. Joy pressed her body more urgently against Carmen and enjoyed every inch of contact as she slid her fingers slowly back and forth. Carmen's breathing got a little faster and coarser as her body responded.

She threw her arms around Joy, thighs squeezing her hips, and Joy pinned her against the side of the tub as she rolled her thumb over her and kept moving her fingers, kissing every inch of Carmen's breasts, neck, and tender lips until she felt the spasms of Carmen's body against her hand and her arms tightening around Joy's shoulders.

Then she melted back into the water and Joy was perfectly content to wrap her arms around Carmen and rest her head on her chest, staring out at the picturesque mountain in front of them. It was still snowing and Carmen's soft skin was no longer prickled with goosebumps. Joy kissed her neck and Carmen returned the gesture, kissing the top of Joy's forehead, then she pushed Joy away, causing a wave of water to slosh over the edge of the tub and spread a little way across the bathroom floor. Carmen pushed her against the other side of the tub, kissing her and ordering her up onto the ledge.

Joy did as she asked, sitting on the edge of the tub with her back resting against the tile wall that had been warmed by the steam from the water. Carmen pulled her hips to the edge of the tub and Joy looked down at her, running one hand along the side of Carmen's perfect face and letting her thumb linger over her plump lower lip.

Then Carmen dipped her head and brought her mouth to Joy's body.

She had to grip the edge of the tub to stay still, to keep from slipping into the water or squirming involuntarily out of Carmen's reach. Her tongue explored her and lit Joy on fire.

❄

JOY WISHED that they could lie together in the tub a while longer. She would have loved to slide back into the water and pull Carmen into her lap, wrapping her arms around her shoulders to protect her from the cold while they watched the snow fall outside.

But they'd pushed their luck as it was – the Castillos could be heading back to the cabin at any moment, and once Joy caught her breath, she realized that it was time for this moment to end. There were a lot of those in her life lately, moments that she'd rather stay in but which had to end, and she pushed the thought aside as she helped Carmen out of the tub and handed her a robe from a stack at the end of the counter.

She toweled off and then got dressed, and while Carmen was standing in front of the mirror to dry her hair, Joy came up behind her and wrapped her arms around her waist. Tomorrow was Christmas Eve, and two days later she'd be gone. There were not enough hours in the world for Joy to get her fill of this girl, but seventy-two sounded like an impossibly small number.

"Hey," she said, kissing Carmen just as she was about

to turn on the hair dryer. "You know what we should do tomorrow after I get off work?"

"What?"

"We should go get a Christmas tree," she said. "There's a tree farm not far outside of Emerald Hill where my parents used to take me when I was a kid. We can check one more thing off your dad's 'white Christmas' bucket list, and I bet your sisters would have fun."

"We already have a tree," Carmen pointed out. "And so do you."

"True," Joy said, letting go of Carmen and leaning up against the counter to watch her dry her hair. She turned the wet ringlets into plump curls, and when she was done, Joy said, "What if we take it to the shelter? They've got an artificial tree, but the thing is ancient and it's starting to look pretty sad."

"Okay," Carmen said. "I think that would be really nice. I bet my dad would be interested to get a look at the food pantry, too. I'm not sure he's stopped thinking about your little organization conundrum since you mentioned it last night."

"Great," Joy said. "My shift ends at five tomorrow. I'll meet you at the cabin, and you just make sure it works with your dad's itinerary."

Carmen laughed, and Joy pulled her into one last, quick kiss before she set about draining the tub and mopping up the overflowed water, making the bathroom look as if they hadn't just taken one of the nicest bubble baths of Joy's life.

DECEMBER 24

TWENTY-THREE
CARMEN

Christmas Eve was a day of anticipation for Carmen, just like it always had been when she was a kid, spending the day eagerly awaiting Santa's arrival. This year, she wasn't waiting for presents or even the holiday itself. She was waiting for Joy to finish her shift, anxious because the closer they got to Christmas Day, the harder it was to ignore the fact that their relationship had an expiration date that was quickly approaching.

She spent the day attempting to distract herself from that fact, volunteering to take Marisol and Maria back to the ski slopes after lunch. They'd found an unexpected aptitude for snowblading yesterday, and Carmen decided that being on the mountain would provide ample diversion for her thoughts while also giving her parents some time to themselves for the first time since they arrived. The twins quickly outgrew the bunny hill and started clamoring to try out the next challenge, a blue square slope, and Carmen went with them a little apprehensively. She watched them take their first ride on the chair lift, following behind them and snow ploughing her way all the way back down the hill while her sisters flew fearlessly in front of her.

They finally made their way back to the cabin around four o'clock, where Mom had cups of hot cocoa waiting to help them warm up. They got changed and the light was beginning to go yellow and muted in the sky by the time Joy pulled into the little driveway in front of the cabin. Carmen's heart leaped into her throat the moment she heard it, and she dashed over to the door to meet her.

"Hey," she said. "I missed you."

It was an understatement, but she still paused for a moment after she said it, wondering if it was too honest. Joy just smiled at her, though, and gave her a quick kiss.

"I missed you, too," she answered when they pulled out of the kiss. "Is everybody ready?"

"Yeah," Carmen said. She led Joy into the cabin, where her family was pulling on their coats, and noticed that Joy was dressed in jeans and a heavy flannel shirt beneath her jacket. Carmen teased, "I didn't realize we were supposed to dress for the part. I left my lumberjack clothes in New York."

"You do know cutting a tree down involves laying on the ground, right?" Joy replied. "I'm dressed appropriately."

"And I have no intention of lying on the ground," Carmen answered. "My dad on the other hand..."

"Ready to go full lumberjack," he said, coming over to

meet Carmen and Joy in the foyer. "Thanks for suggesting this. It's a great tradition that our family seems to have gotten away from."

Mom and the twins joined the group and Joy said, "I borrowed one of the resort's transport vans for tonight. Everyone ready?"

"Ready," Marisol said as Mom adjusted her scarf a little tighter around her face and she gave her a look of mild annoyance.

They all climbed into the van, Carmen in front with Joy, then Mom and Dad, and the twins in the back. Mom leaned forward to talk to Joy as they drove, thanking her for the ski lesson the day before and telling her how eager the twins had been to get back out on the slopes again today.

"We really should have gotten out there from the start," she said. "We'll have to come back again next year because I think the girls have been bitten by the skiing bug."

Joy glanced over at Carmen and she could read what was in her eyes – the promise of seeing each other again, mixed with a little bit of agony over the fact that Mom was talking about next Christmas, three hundred and sixty-six days away.

Carmen reached across the space between their seats and squeezed Joy's hand, then said, "You would have been proud of us – we made it all the way down a blue square hill and only one of us fell down. Guess who?"

Joy laughed and said, "But you got away unscathed this time, so that's an improvement."

"Hah," Carmen said. "I didn't fall - it was Marisol because she's fearless and doesn't believe in snow ploughing."

"I may have fallen, but it took *you* twenty minutes to get down the hill," Marisol called from the back of the van, and Mom and Joy both laughed at Carmen's expense.

The tree farm was about a twenty-minute drive away from the resort, through the town of Emerald Hill, and just to the edge of the mountain where the ground started to level out and make way for a small, forested area. It was dusk by the time Joy pulled the van into a gravel parking lot that was lit with twinkling white string lights on poles all around the perimeter, and there were only a few cars in the parking lot.

"Here we are," Joy said as she came to a stop in front of a small log cabin that acted as the tree farm's office as well as a small Christmas shop.

Everyone got out of the van and Joy walked over, slipping her gloved hand into Carmen's. There was a split rail fence along one side of the shop with about twenty-five pre-cut trees leaning against it, all of them already bound with twine for any last-minute tree shoppers who didn't have the time or desire to cut their own. The shop itself was decorated with twinkling Christmas lights, and a delightful mix of pine and cinnamon wafted into the air as the front door opened and a man in overalls and a flannel shirt came out.

"Hey, folks, you looking for a pre-cut tree?"

"We'd like to cut our own," Dad said. "Is it too late for that?"

"Not at all," the man said. "But it's getting dark so you better hurry up."

He pointed them to the end of the fence, where about a dozen hacksaws hung from a post, and the same number of deep plastic sleds were stacked together.

"Grab a sled and a hacksaw and have at it," he said. "You folks been here before?"

"I have," Joy said. "But it's been a long time."

The man nodded and pointed to the field behind the shop, where a couple acres of pine trees were growing in neat lines. He told them where they could find the different species of trees, and the prices for each, and then he set them loose to begin the hunt.

"When you're done, come into the shop and I'll help you get 'er tied to your van," he said. "We also got ornaments and hot cocoa and fresh candied almonds if I can tempt ya."

The Castillos headed into the field, walking single-file through the rows of trees. There was just enough light left in the sky to let them find what they were looking for among the stout, full-branched Douglas firs and the regal-looking Norwegian spruce trees. Most of them had a light dusting of snow on them, and the walking was slow because there was at least five inches on the ground.

Carmen linked her arm in Joy's and they followed behind the rest of the family. She didn't pay attention to any tree in particular, enjoying the moment instead.

They lingered and fell further and further behind everyone else, and when they found themselves separated from the rest of the family by at least two dozen trees, Joy stopped Carmen to kiss her.

"Are you having a good Christmas Eve?" she asked.

"The best," Carmen answered, and then she took out her phone and made Joy pose for a couple more photos, using the trees and the mountains as the background. It was a much better shot than the one she'd been trying to take when Joy came over that hill and smashed into her, and she would enjoy looking at it a lot more than a picture that was taken simply to prove a point to Brigid and her annoying new boyfriend.

Carmen wanted as many mementos as she could get to remember her by, and she smiled a little as she noticed the number of notifications that had gone unseen since the last time she took out her phone. On any other vacation, in any other place than at the base of the magical Emerald Mountain, Carmen's fingers would have been itching to check on her best friend and find out everything that she was missing. This place had changed her though – *Joy* had changed her – and it all seemed rather inconsequential to her now.

She slid her phone back into her pocket and took Joy's hand, and they started walking again, trying to catch up with the rest of her family. Carmen pointed out a few pretty trees here and there as they went, and Joy let her know what was wrong with each one.

"The trunk is too crooked, it'll never stand up," she

said about one, and, "There's a dead branch – it's probably got a disease."

"Killjoy," Carmen said after a few more of Joy's criticisms, knocking into her with her shoulder. "If you're the tree expert, why don't you pick a good one?"

"I just have more experience at this than you do," Joy said. "I can't count the number of times I've brought a tree home because it was full and green and lovely, but the trunk was crooked and we had to spend the entire month trying to keep it from falling over. My dad got so sick of it one year that he tied the whole damn tree to the window sash."

Carmen laughed and was about to point out another one when they heard her dad calling from further down the row, "Get over here, girls, I think we found the one!"

The winning tree turned out to be a seven-foot-tall Fraser fir, its branches perfectly even and green and its shape the epitome of Christmas trees. As soon as everyone agreed that it was the prettiest one on the lot – or at least the prettiest one they would find before dark settled in and made the task all the more tricky – Dad took the hacksaw and climbed under the tree.

"Can somebody hold it steady?" he called, his voice slightly muffled from the thick needles above his head.

"Go ahead," Joy said, nudging Carmen forward.

She reached into the thick branches, the needles slightly prickly even through her gloves, and grabbed onto the trunk while Dad worked the saw back and forth at the tree's base. It took a good five minutes for him to saw all the way through, partly because Maria decided she wanted to take a whack at it, too. Then he called, "Timber!" and told Carmen to let go. The tree fell onto the sled, snow coming off it in a cloud.

"I think we did pretty well," Dad said with a grin, and Mom linked her arm in his.

"It's a good tree," she said. "If we're going to take it to the shelter, we'll need to buy a stand and some ornaments."

"They've got ornaments there," Joy said. "We can take them off the artificial tree."

"No," Mom said, "we'll leave them both up, and see what kind of ornaments are in the shop."

So they went back up the rows of trees and found the man in the overalls waiting for them.

"Find a good one?" he asked.

"I think so," Dad said. "Can you tie it up for us?"

Mom and the twins went inside the shop to pick out some ornaments and Carmen stood beside Joy, watching with wonder as the man lifted their tree out of the sled and took it over to a small metal box on the ground, kicking a switch to turn it on. He put the trunk of the tree on top of a vibrating metal plate on top of the box and it shook all the loose needles almost violently out of the tree, and then he carried the freshly cleaned tree over to another machine, which he fed it through in order to wrap it tightly in twine.

He and Dad managed to get it hoisted onto the top of the van and tied it to the luggage rack with more twine, then they all went inside to settle the bill. Carmen and Joy picked out a few ornaments – Carmen was drawn to a pair of ceramic turtle doves that she set in Joy's palm with a kiss on her cheek – and the man wrapped them all up in brown paper and packed them in gift bags. Then they thanked him and everyone climbed back into the van for the short trip over to the shelter.

It was just past dinnertime when they got there and the people who would be making use of the shelter's cots to stay warm overnight were helping Tyler and a few other volunteers to clean up the kitchen after their meal. Joy told Tyler about the tree that she and the Castillos had gotten for the shelter and he pointed them to an area of the great room that would be a good spot for it, near the door and the front window of the shelter. A few shelter visitors came outside to help Carmen's dad get the tree down from the roof of the van, and then they all worked together on making room and setting up the tree.

Joy and Carmen carefully moved the artificial tree to the other side of the great room, near the entrance to the food pantry, and Maria and Marisol followed behind them, picking up the ornaments that dropped off its limbs as they carried it. Dad and one of the visitors worked together to level the cut bottom of the new tree, then put it into the stand that they'd purchased at the Christmas shop, and Mom went into the kitchen to fetch a pitcher of water for it. Then they carefully unwrapped all of the ornaments and garlands they had bought, laying them out on a table not far away.

The Castillos stepped aside for the shelter visitors to take over decorating the tree, and Joy sat down on the table, pulling Carmen between her legs and wrapping her arms around her waist while they watched. There were a couple of kids staying at the shelter that night and their eyes lit up as soon as they realized that they were being tasked with trimming the tree. Carmen put her hands on top of Joy's while she watched the kids' parents lifting them up, helping them reach the higher branches to place their ornaments.

She saw one of them pick up the turtle dove ornament that she'd chosen, hanging it delicately in the center of the tree, and she leaned back to kiss Joy on the cheek. She said, "Thank you for suggesting this. It's so much more special than a Cancun Christmas spent shopping til we drop."

"Thank you for thinking it was a good idea," Joy answered, holding her a little tighter.

After the tree was decorated and the lights were turned on, twinkling with every color and casting the room in a festive glow, Dad came over to Carmen and Joy and said, "Let's have a look at that food pantry, shall we?"

"Sure," Joy said, releasing Carmen and sliding off the table.

She took him across the room to the pantry, Carmen following behind them, and she was right about the problem – it had only been a few days, but more donations had obviously come in and the shelves were beginning to look chaotic again already.

"Far be it for me to complain about people's generosity," Joy said as she walked Dad through the space and explained the issue, "but it can get pretty difficult to make sure everyone's getting what they need and nothing's going to waste when we can't even keep the room organized."

"I see your dilemma," Dad said, back in his pondering state with his hand on his chin.

He walked around the room a few times, getting a feel for the dimensions of the space and reading the worn labels that Joy, or some other volunteer, had put on the shelves in an effort to fix the problem. Carmen and Joy stood in the doorway, practically watching the gears in his mind turn, until Tyler appeared in the doorway.

"Hey," he said. "Whatcha up to?"

"Carmen's dad thinks he might be able to fix our disorderly food pantry problem," Joy said.

"Oh, that would be amazing," Tyler said. Then he turned to Carmen and said, "You're staying after Christmas, right? Moving here and taking this place on full-time?"

Carmen blushed and her eyes darted to Joy. Staying here – that was the fantasy that kept running through her mind over the last few days, but of course she couldn't do that. Her life was in New York, and she'd only met Joy a week ago. It was crazy to even think about it.

"Because you've been a godsend," Tyler went on. "I might just have to kidnap you for the good of the shelter."

Carmen laughed and Joy put her arm around Carmen's shoulder. Dad came and joined them, introducing himself to Tyler and shaking hands. He said, "No genius ideas yet, but I'm sure there must be a solution."

"You've done more than enough already," Tyler said. "I'm looking forward to serving a hot meal to all these folks in the morning so I don't have to tell them they're spending most of Christmas Day with empty stomachs."

"Don't give me credit," Dad said. "That was all Carmen's idea."

"I don't mean to push my luck," Tyler said as Mom and the twins came over to meet them and see what all the activity was about in the food pantry, "but would any of you like to come back in the morning and help me serve the meal? We could always use a few extra hands."

"Oh, I'm sure they've got a lot to keep them busy tomorrow," Joy started to say, but Mom cut her off.

"We'd be happy to," she said. "I don't know if Carmen told you, but we made use of a food pantry a number of times when she was younger. I think it'd be a really nice thing for us to do as a family, and the twins might appreciate all the presents waiting under the tree for them a bit more if they have to delay gratification for a few hours."

"Really?" Tyler asked, like he hadn't expected his request to be granted. "Thank you, we certainly appreciate it."

"No problem," Dad said. "We'll be here with bells on."

TWENTY-FOUR

JOY

Joy drove the Castillos back to the cabin shortly after Tyler convinced them to come to the shelter again in the morning to help with breakfast, and when she tried to drop them off at the door, Carmen said, "Where do you think you're going?"

"To drop off the van and then go back to my apartment?" Joy asked while the rest of the Castillos climbed out of the van and went inside.

"No way," Carmen said. She reached over and turned the key in the ignition, saying, "You're not going to spend Christmas Eve alone. Come inside, we're going to unwrap presents."

"Oh, well, I should go home then," Joy objected. "This is your time to be with your family."

"I don't want to be anywhere you aren't," Carmen said. Then in a sing-song voice she added, "There's a gift for you under the tree."

Joy smiled and followed Carmen into the cabin –

although she didn't have much of a choice since Carmen had taken the van's key out of the ignition and slipped it into her coat pocket. Inside, the twins were shedding their heavy winter coats and Lucia was in the kitchen, heating milk for a round of hot cocoas. Tony was wearing a Santa hat and heading over to the tree to start distributing presents, and suddenly Joy felt a pang of nostalgia. Apparently, it made no difference whether you grew up in a tiny house in the bad part of town, or a quaint mountainside village, or in a New York penthouse – the spirit of Christmas felt the same in every family.

Joy sank contentedly into the lounge chair and Carmen crawled into it with her, their hips pressing together on the cushion that wasn't quite big enough for two. She wrapped her arms around Carmen and watched as the twins pointed at various gift-wrapped boxes beneath the tree and begged their dad to pick them first.

"Hmm," he was saying as he poked around under the tree, hunting for the right gift to give each of them. "What do we have here?"

He gave Marisol a long, flat package, and handed Maria a small box with a red ribbon on top. They tore into them with glee, and Carmen leaned into Joy, resting her head against her as she explained, "They know what's in most of those boxes. They buy what they want with their Christmas allowance and then we wrap it and put it all under the tree. They're at the age where it's mostly clothes, so I hope you don't mind getting a fashion show once they open everything."

"Sounds cute," Joy said with a laugh. "A little bit redundant, but cute."

"Santa will come tonight and leave them a couple things that they *don't* already know about," Lucia said as she came over and set down a couple mugs of cocoa on the table beside Carmen and Joy. She lowered her voice, although it didn't matter because the twins were totally absorbed in unwrapping their gifts, and added with a wink, "They're too old to believe in Santa Claus *except* when it comes to getting extra presents."

Joy and Carmen sat for a while, watching the girls become buried in a growing mound of torn wrapping paper and wrinkled tissue paper. Tony was having great fun playing Santa, handing a few things to his wife and eldest daughter here and there, and then he pulled a large, oblong package out from behind the tree and said in his best low-pitched Santa voice, "Oh, and this one's for Joy. Ho ho ho."

He brought it over to her and she set down her mug, scooting over to the ottoman to handle the large present. It was nearly as tall as she was, wrapped in beautiful gold paper with tiny snowflakes printed on it, and she looked skeptically at Carmen. "This is for me?"

"Yeah," Carmen said, nudging the box toward her.

"You didn't have to do this," Joy objected.

"I wanted to," Carmen said. "Open it."

Joy smiled, leaned in to kiss her, and then she carefully opened the wrapping paper. It was a very beautiful, very expensive snowboard and a new set of bindings, and she looked at Carmen open-mouthed as she peeled back the rest of the wrapping paper.

"And I *did* have to do it," Carmen said, putting her arms around Joy and not giving her a chance to voice further objection. It really was an elaborate gift, and Joy could feel the eyes of the rest of the Castillos on her, smiling and watching the two of them. Carmen reminded her, "I broke your other board."

"Just the binding," Joy said. "It'll be an easy repair."

"Well, now you have two snowboards to choose from, then," Carmen said with a shrug.

"Thank you," Joy answered. "I love it."

"You're welcome," Carmen said, kissing her quickly while Tony went back to handing out presents to the twins.

Joy took the snowboard out of its box, inspecting the design and the smooth finish. Lucia came over and took a look as well, telling her that it had been the prettiest one in the ski shop when she and Carmen went to shop for her. Then she went and handed her husband a present, telling him to sit down and relax for a minute, and Joy sank back into the couch with Carmen, putting her arm around her.

"I got you something, too," she said. "But it's barely a gift – more like a memento. I think I shouldn't even bother giving it to you after you gave me that beautiful snowboard."

"You don't need to get me anything at all," Carmen said. "Unless you've got more time. Can you turn tonight into another week and a half?"

"No," Joy said sadly. Then she got up and held out her hand to Carmen. "Come with me - it's in the van. I wasn't sure when I'd get a chance to give it to you."

They put their coats on and went outside, the rest of Carmen's family hardly even noticing their absence. It was dark and cold, and Carmen crossed her arms in front of her chest and started shivering almost immediately. Joy never really minded the cold – she was accustomed to it – but she always loved it when she found herself outside on nights when the rest of Emerald Hill was indoors. It was so peaceful and serene to feel like the only person on the mountainside, but now – at least for a little while longer – she got to share that feeling with Carmen.

They went around to the back of the van and she opened the door, helping Carmen climb inside and then closing the door again to protect them from the wind. It was only marginally warmer there, but sitting in the cargo area behind the back seat was a small package wrapped in green and red paper. Joy sat down across from Carmen, picking it up and handing it to her.

"Here," she said, apologizing before Carmen had even unwrapped it. "Like I said, it's not much."

Carmen looked at her, leaned over in the space between them to kiss her, and then opened it. There was a small cardboard box, about five inches square, which Joy had nabbed from the tea party at the lodge the other day. It had a picture of a teapot on the side of it, but it was really the perfect size for the gift she'd known would be perfect for Carmen since their first encounter on the side of the mountain.

It was a snow globe, heavy and filled with light flakes of glitter dressed up as snow. There was a mountain with a little cabin nestled into its side, the roof covered in snow and a great big Christmas tree beside it.

"It's beautiful," Carmen said, giving it a shake and sending the snow swirling down around the cabin.

"Look," Joy said, leaning in to point out a pair of tiny skiers on the side of the mountain, barely larger than a couple crystals of sugar. "It's us."

"Except they're not crashing into each other," Carmen said, grinning at her.

Her voice had a slightly watery quality about it, and Joy thought that if they sat in this empty van much longer, she was either going to cry or try to seduce Carmen. It could go either way, but with her family just inside the cabin, neither was right. She said, "Umm, it belonged to my dad, so take care of it, okay?"

"It did?" Carmen asked, surprised. "You can't give this to me."

"I want you to have it," Joy said. "It's yours. Besides, I've got at least ten more at home – he was a collector. So anyway, we better get you back inside before you freeze."

She opened the door to the van, eager to get out before she really did start bawling like a baby, and they headed back into the cabin. She thought she should excuse herself soon, although the dark, empty apartment wasn't exactly beckoning to her. She would just go inside and say goodnight to everyone, then let them have the rest of their Christmas Eve to themselves.

But when they got inside, the twins were just beginning their fashion show, marching through the center of the living room in a pair of matching parkas, and Tony's eyes lit up the moment he saw Joy coming back in.

"Joy, I just had a breakthrough!" he exclaimed, rushing over to her. "I think I know how to fix the pantry problem."

He was elated, and Carmen squeezed Joy's hand as he led them both over to the dining table, where he'd scribbled a few notes on the back of one of his itinerary pages.

"It's all about inventory control," he said. "So what if we re-arrange the shelves a little bit and install a barcode reader at the door? You feed the cans in and the reader sends them to the appropriate place via a series of chutes..."

Tony explained his idea in depth, sketching it out roughly on the paper while his eyes shone with excitement, and he promised to find someone in the Denver area that could help Tyler make his invention into reality. Then when he was done explaining it all, they went back into the living room and watched the twins continue their fashion show, complete with costume changes and a makeshift runway down the center of the living room.

When it got late and everyone was yawning, Marisol and Maria having fallen asleep at the end of the couch and still wearing the last wardrobe items in their show, Tony and Lucia carried them into their bedroom and Joy said again, "I should go home."

"You *are* home," Carmen said. "At least for tonight. Stay with me."

"Your parents won't mind?" Joy asked.

"I'm sure they would insist on it if they knew the alternative was waking up to an empty apartment on Christmas morning," Carmen said. "Come on, I'll give you some of my pajamas to sleep in."

She took Joy's hand and led her down the hall, and it felt like a dream to curl up in the big, soft bed with her. Joy fell asleep easier in Carmen's arms than she had in a long time, and visions of a happily ever after danced in her head.

DECEMBER 25

TWENTY-FIVE

CARMEN

Carmen woke up early on Christmas morning, the soft pink notes of the sunrise coloring the sky outside her window. She could hear her parents moving around in the cabin, probably making breakfast or putting the finishing touches on the gifts that Santa had left beneath the tree, and soon it would be time to go to the shelter and help with breakfast.

For the moment, though, she was content to lie still to keep from waking Joy. She was nestled in the crook of Carmen's arm, and even though her hand was tingling with numbness, she didn't want to move her – she just wanted to watch her sleep. Carmen looked at the snow globe that Joy had given her the night before, which had belonged to her father and which was already very special to Carmen. She'd given it pride of place on the bedside table, setting it just beside her phone so that she wouldn't forget to pack it when it was time to go back to

New York. All the snow had settled in it now, coating the bottom of the little scene with glittering white flakes.

Joy stirred when someone shut a cupboard in the kitchen, then sleepily looked up at Carmen.

"Good morning," she said, her lips forming into an only half-roused smile that Carmen wanted to put in her pocket and keep.

"Merry Christmas," Carmen corrected, rolling Joy over on her back and kissing her passionately. They didn't get a chance to get too deep into this moment, though, because a moment later there was a knock on the door.

"Up and at 'em," Dad called. "We've got to head out soon if we're going to get to the shelter on time to serve breakfast."

Joy grinned at Carmen, clearly just as agonized by the interruption as she was, then said, "Merry Christmas," and rolled out of the bed. Carmen loaned Joy a pair of jeans and a sweater so she wouldn't have to wear her lumberjack clothes again today, and then they joined the rest of the family in the living room. Mom had made coffee and handed them each a travel mug, which Carmen gratefully accepted, and Dad was still wearing his Santa hat. Then they all headed for the door, the twins carrying a wrapped gift from beneath the tree under each arm.

"What're they up to?" Carmen asked as they went out to the van.

"They wanted to donate a couple of their presents to

the kids at the shelter," Mom said. "I told them it sounded like a nice gesture and Santa would approve."

※

WHEN THEY ARRIVED at the shelter, a handful of other volunteers were just beginning to cook. Those who had stayed overnight at the shelter were waking up in the great room, stacking their cots out of the way and helping Tyler to set up the folding tables they used for meals. Both trees were lit and the whole space smelled like pine and Christmas.

"Hey, thanks for coming," Tyler said with a wave as soon as the Castillos came in.

"Happy to help," Dad said. "Where do you need us?"

"Check in with Marty in the kitchen," he said. "She'll tell you where she needs assistance."

Joy showed them the way, leading them to a small hallway leading off the great room and then into the kitchen which was already hectic with the cooking efforts. Marty and two other women were scrambling eggs and putting bread into pans to toast, and it seemed almost a nuisance to stop them in order to ask how they could help.

"Hey, Mart," Joy said. "I brought reinforcements. What do you need?"

Marty gave them each tasks, then went back to her eggs. Dad went back into the great room to help Tyler with his table setup, Carmen and Joy stayed in the kitchen to peel potatoes and slice them thin for hash browns, and Mom and the twins went to set up the buffet table where the food would be served. It was hectic and Carmen found herself breaking a sweat in the hot kitchen but every time she looked over at Joy absorbed in her task, her heart felt full and she didn't want to be anywhere else.

It was about ten minutes to eight when Tyler came into the kitchen to help them carry the chafing dishes full of eggs, potatoes and bacon into the great room where they'd be served. Carmen and Joy lined up behind the buffet table, along with the rest of the Castillo family, and spent the next half an hour serving up food and wishing people a Merry Christmas. Most of them had big smiles on their faces and it made Carmen feel warm and fuzzy to watch how they licked their lips and looked eagerly at their meals. It was unlike any Christmas she'd had before, and with Joy standing beside her, she was sure that it was her best one yet.

Once everyone got their food and had gone to the tables to eat, Dad had a good time circulating through the room, talking to everyone and telling them his rags to riches story, omitting of course the little detail of how his famous app had been born of laziness and a desire to get his friends to fetch him alcohol. Carmen had to smile at this omission as she overheard him saying to one table, "I had to hit bottom before I had the freedom to start climbing back out of that hole. You just do what you can and take it one day at a time, and things will get better."

She helped Joy and the other volunteers clean up the breakfast mess, and then she watched the twins bring their presents over to the kids they'd met yesterday. Their eyes lit up the moment they realized the gifts were for them, and then she watched with amusement as their eyes darted over to Dad in his Santa hat. They may have been a few years younger than Marisol and Maria, but they were already skeptical of the idea of a fat man in a red suit handing things out for free. They were just opening the presents, some warm weather clothes mixed with a few books that the twins had been dying to read, when Joy came up and grabbed Carmen's hand.

"Come with me," she said, pulling her away from the buffet table.

"Where are we going?" Carmen asked.

Instead of answering, Joy just led her into the food pantry and shut the door, pulling her into a tight embrace. They kissed, and in between moments when their lips were locked, Joy murmured against Carmen's skin, "I have to go to work soon. I wish I didn't have to leave you."

"I wish I wasn't going back to New York tomorrow," Carmen said.

"Don't say that," Joy said. "Let me pretend that isn't happening."

They kissed again, Carmen's pulse quickening and her body responding to Joy's closeness, and it was hard to forget even though Joy's lips made a good argument for it. This time tomorrow, Carmen would be packing her bags. By noon she'd be in Denver, and by dinnertime she'd be back in New York, back to her old life.

Joy was right – it was best to push those thoughts out

of her head and stay in the moment instead. She did her best to focus all of her attention on the way that Joy's lips felt against hers, the shivery sensations that overtook her every time Joy touched her, and the aching way that her heart demanded she stay as close as possible to Joy for as long as she could. She wondered if Joy would mind if she just followed her around the resort all day today, and if her parents would understand.

Then there was a knock on the door and they stepped away from each other, straightening their clothes as Tyler came in.

"Am I interrupting something?" he asked with a smirk. "I just needed to get a bag of dried beans for dinner tonight."

"No, come in," Joy said. "We're going to head out because I've got to get to work."

"Okay, well, thanks again for all of your help," Tyler said, shaking Carmen's hand. "Everyone really appreciated the breakfast and it was a big help that you guys took the time to come lend a hand this morning."

"It's our pleasure," Carmen said, feeling safe to speak for the rest of her family as well. "Merry Christmas, Tyler."

"Merry Christmas," he said. "Joy, I'll see you next week?"

"Yeah," Joy said. "Mr. Castillo had some interesting ideas about the food pantry. I'll fill you in then."

Carmen and Joy found the rest of the family still mingling with the shelter visitors and volunteers, and the kids that Marisol and Maria had made friends with were already absorbed in their new books. Joy told them that she had to get to work soon so they all piled back into the van and she drove them to the cabin. During the ride, they talked about their own Christmas Day tradition, which had Carmen salivating already.

"None of us particularly enjoys spending the day in the kitchen," she explained to Joy, "so we order food for Christmas. It started out pretty reasonable, catering from one restaurant, and over the years we've tried so many different dishes and found so many awesome things that we started ordering from a bunch of different places so that everyone can have their favorite food on the holiday."

"Dad and I usually go for traditional Mexican dishes – plantains, Johnnycakes, and sea food – but Carmen's used to more American fare like ham, mashed potatoes, and stuffing," Mom added. "And the twins insist on a variety of desserts."

"Sounds delicious," Joy said, then added with a laugh, "and excessive."

"Trust me, none of it goes to waste," Dad said with another festive belly laugh.

"What's your favorite Christmas dish?" Mom asks Joy. "We'll order it for you and have it ready when you're done with work."

"Oh," Joy said, pausing to think for a minute. "Mince pies. My mom makes them and they're incredible."

"I'll be sure to get you some," Mom said, not accepting Joy's objections. Finally, as they pulled up to the cabin, she relented and thanked Carmen's mom.

Then they all climbed out of the van except for Joy, and Carmen stayed with her in the front seat.

"I'll come inside in a minute," Carmen called as the rest of her family went into the cabin, the twins eager to open the last of their gifts waiting beneath the tree. Carmen thought about asking Joy if she could tag along on her shift, but instead she just leaned across the aisle and kissed her. Then she looked at the clock on the dashboard and said, "I'm leaving in twenty-four hours exactly."

TWENTY-SIX

JOY

"I know," Joy said with a sigh. She kissed Carmen again, but there were only so many times that would work to distract her from the fact that she'd somehow managed to fall for a girl who she knew she'd never see again. Her heart was already heavy with that knowledge.

"So you're coming straight over after work, right?" Carmen asked. "My mom wasn't kidding about those mince pies – they'll be waiting for you, and if you want a break during your shift, I can bring you one as soon as they get here."

Joy laughed and gave Carmen a smile, doing her best to disguise the sadness beneath it. She couldn't help but think that if Danny hadn't left Emerald Hill, she probably never would have fallen so hard for Carmen. She would have kept busy with her job and her volunteer work and her best friend and she might not have been on the slopes at all they day that Carmen crashed into her life. Even if they had met, Danny probably would have been able to keep her grounded, to remind her that Carmen was painfully temporary.

And now she had to learn that lesson all by herself.

Painfully.

The idea of making this their last moment together had started to form in Joy's mind at the shelter. She was stealing surreptitious glances at Carmen, memorizing the barely discernible dimples that formed in her cheeks every time she smiled and wished someone a Merry Christmas, thinking about how she hadn't noticed those dimples before and there was no use learning new things about Carmen so late in their fleeting relationship. That was when she really started thinking about the moment when they would have to say goodbye to each other.

She would come back over to the Castillo cabin after her shift tonight and they'd have Christmas dinner together. Carmen was persuasive and Joy's defenses had been thoroughly lowered by now, so she would almost definitely spend the night again. Then in the morning she would have to sit helplessly and watch Carmen pack her bags and prepare to walk out on her forever. Joy hated that idea, and she hated even the mental image of watching Carmen walking away from her, wondering if she would look back at her one last time.

So by the time she dropped Carmen and the rest of her family back at the cabin, Joy was pretty certain that this would be the last time she saw her. It would be better this way, ending what should have been a carefree fling on a happy moment and keeping that as their last memory together. Joy didn't want to see Carmen sad, and she didn't want to show her how hard it was not to cry at the thought of losing her, so they would end on an optimistic moment instead.

"I'll be done around six if I'm lucky," she said. "Maybe longer if it's a crazy day, which Christmas often is."

"Okay," Carmen said. "Come right over after."

Joy put her hand out and Carmen took it, and Joy brought her fingers to her lips. She wasn't wearing her gloves and they were cold, so Joy took a minute to blow on them, rubbing them between her fingers to warm her up. Then she leaned across the space between their seats and kissed her, saying, "Merry Christmas, Carmen."

"Merry Christmas, Joy," Carmen repeated back to her. "I'll see you soon."

"Okay," Joy croaked, and then Carmen was gone. She watched her walk into the cabin, then drove the short distance down to the lodge. She was holding back tears that came out of nowhere – it felt absurd to be this broken up about a girl she just met – and just as she was sitting in the parking lot and trying to pull herself together so she could go inside and start her shift, her phone started ringing.

Joy's heart skipped a beat and she let out a sigh as she dug it out of her pocket. She figured it was Carmen, calling to ask a question about the mince pies for her mother or something like that, and Joy didn't think she had the energy to lie to her again. It had taken every ounce of her courage to do it the first time without breaking down and telling Carmen that she'd screwed up and fallen for her, and she knew it would do more harm than good to admit that out loud.

Instead of Carmen calling, though, it was Joy's mother.

"Hey, sweetie," she said as soon as Joy picked up. "I wasn't expecting you to answer - I was going to leave a voicemail to wish you a Merry Christmas. Are you working today?"

"Yeah," Joy said, "just about to go clock in."

"Okay, I won't keep you then," Mom started to say, but then she caught the watery quality of Joy's voice, which she'd tried her best to disguise. Her mom always noticed that stuff, though, especially over the phone when her voice was all she had. "Something wrong?"

"No," Joy tried to lie, but then she found herself spilling everything to her mother. She didn't want to keep it inside herself any longer, and she didn't know how she'd make it through the day if she didn't tell someone what was eating her. The time clock could wait, and she said, "I met a girl at the resort last week."

She told her mother about their ill-fated meeting on the black diamond hill, and how immediately they had clicked. She told her how fascinating Carmen and her family were, and all the different layers she'd managed to peel back that turned them from the average rich resort guests into a family that she'd really connected with this week. And of course, Joy couldn't tell the story without telling her mother how magnetic Carmen seemed to be, pulling her closer with every day and leaving her with the feeling that her heart might burst the moment she left Emerald Hill.

"I got attached to her and I knew it was a bad idea," Joy said, frustrated and on the verge of tears.

"Sweetie," Mom said sympathetically, "love isn't a matter of choice. You can't just *decide* not to have feelings for someone."

"I know," Joy said helplessly.

"Does she know how you feel?" Mom asked, and the idea of having that conversation with Carmen struck all her most painful heartstrings.

"I can't imagine that she doesn't," she said. "But we haven't exactly talked about it."

"You should," her mom said.

"Why? She's getting on a plane tomorrow," Joy said. "She lives on the other side of the country and there's nothing I can do about the fact that I stupidly allowed myself to fall for her."

"You don't know that," Mom said. "If she's got you this emotional, then you should tell her before it really is too late. It can't hurt to talk."

"It might," Joy said. In fact, she was sure that it would, that Carmen would confirm all her darkest fears by telling her that she was going to have no trouble getting over her, or worse, that she cared about Joy too but it didn't matter and she was going back to her lavish lifestyle in New York anyway. Joy wiped an errant tear from her cheek and changed the subject, asking, "Did you and Allen go see the Christmas displays at Disney?"

Mom laughed and said, "Wouldn't you know it? We didn't get around to it again this year."

"Mom!" Joy said, laughing with her. "It's probably not too late. You should go today."

"Maybe we will," she said. Then after a little pause in which Joy checked the mirror in the back of the visor and saw that her eyes were a little bit red from trying unsuccessfully to hold in her tears, Mom added, "Don't let this turn into something you regret, sweetie. Take a leap of faith and tell her how you feel."

"Thanks, Mom," Joy said, taking a deep breath. It was a nice pep talk, but she still didn't know if she had the courage to take her mom's advice. "I should get to work."

"Okay," Mom said. "Merry Christmas, sweetie."

"Merry Christmas, Mom," Joy said. "I'll see you in a couple of weeks."

"Looking forward to it," Mom said, and then they hung up and Joy went inside, returning the keys to the van at long last to the transportation office.

"About damn time," the guy at the desk said, joking with her.

Joy wasn't quite in the mood for jokes yet, though, and she nodded at the green elf hat he was wearing. "Nice hat."

"Thanks," he said. "Yours is in your locker."

"Crap," Joy said, but she couldn't help smiling a little bit at the irony.

TWENTY-SEVEN
CARMEN

Christmas dinner on Emerald Mountain turned out to be just as elaborate and exotic as it always was in Cancun. Carmen's mom ordered about a dozen different dishes from the resort's extensive menu, and earlier in the week she'd tasked the twins with finding Emerald Hill's bakery and figuring out what they wanted to order from there for dessert. Dad called a car to take him to pick it up around noon, and he came back with his arms full of boxes containing everything from chocolate cake to puff pastries and fruit tarts.

"Good news," he said as he laid them all out on the kitchen island. "They had little mince pies in their grab-and-go case so I picked up one for each of us."

Carmen texted Joy, snapping a picture of the six perfectly round pies in their bakery box to entice her, and asked whether she wanted her dessert early. She offered, "I can come by the lodge and drop it off if you're hungry."

It was about fifteen minutes before Joy responded,

and Carmen was disappointed to see that she'd answered negatively.

> *I appreciate the offer but we're so busy with room service requests and a banquet going on in the ballroom. I'll just have to be a good girl and wait.*

Carmen couldn't resist the urge to send back a teasing comment about Joy's assertion that she was a good girl, but when Joy didn't respond, she figured that she'd gotten swept up in her work. The rest of her family was already eating – it was only a bit past lunchtime by the time the twins had finished opening their gifts from Santa and everyone's stomachs started rumbling, and it was their tradition to graze and nibble at the feast all day long. Carmen made herself a plate, piling on the mashed potatoes and green bean casserole as well as the cornbread-like Johnnycakes that were Mom's favorite, then went into the living room and sat down in the lounge chair to eat while Dad found *A Christmas Story* playing on television.

She polished off her plate and then lay back in the deep chair, her feet up on the ottoman, to watch the movie and wait for Joy. She kept her phone in her lap in case Joy called or texted and it vibrated again and again as a stream of Merry Christmases and other notifications came through. Carmen looked at a few of them – more beaches and bikini selfies from Brigid and Bentley, and a few dozen social media posts from the rest of her New

York crowd sharing their Christmas gifts in humble brag form.

She sent Brigid a text, a quick one wishing her a Merry Christmas and telling her that she hoped she was having a nice time with Bentley, and found that she meant it for the first time ever. If Bentley made Brigid happy, for whatever reason there could be, then Carmen couldn't stand in the way of that.

Then she put her phone on the arm of the chair and turned her attention back to the television. The rest of her family was doing the same, Dad nodding off and the twins splitting their attention between the movie and a game that Santa had left them, and Mom cleaning up the kitchen. Carmen dozed off too, thinking that sleep was a perfectly good way to while away the hours until she could be with Joy again. If her subconscious was kind to her, then her dreams wouldn't be about the clock ticking down on their time together, or the seventeen hundred miles that would separate them when she got back to New York.

❋

CARMEN WOKE up to the sounds of her parents moving around in the kitchen, heating up plates for another round of their favorite foods. The movie had switched over from *A Christmas Story* to *It's a Wonderful Life,* and she was surprised to see that it was dark outside the big picture window. She sat up abruptly, taking her phone off the arm of the chair and checking her messages.

She found an answer from Brigid in the form of a selfie – Bentley's arm around her shoulders possessively – and a few more social media notifications, but nothing from Joy, and it was past seven o'clock.

"You want some more ham and mashed potatoes?" Mom called to her from the kitchen when she saw that Carmen was awake, and Carmen climbed out of the chair, wiping the sleep from her eyes.

"No," she said. "You guys let me take a four-hour nap?"

"You looked tired," Dad said. "Besides, we all conked out for a little while there. That's what Christmas Day is all about – eating yourself into a coma."

Mom laughed but Carmen felt a little stone of worry settling into her stomach. She knew that Joy said she might have to work later if it was busy, but she didn't think she meant a whole hour later. She thought that Joy would find an excuse to leave so they could spend their precious few remaining hours together.

"I'm going to call Joy," she said, heading into her room and closing the door.

She dialed her number, but there was no answer, and somewhere in the back of her mind she started to worry that Joy was avoiding her. It was silly – she had no reason to think that – but Joy had always found time for Carmen every time she wanted her this week, even when she was busy with work, so where the hell was she now?

When Carmen emerged from the bedroom, Mom asked, "Did you get ahold of her?"

"I don't know how much longer this mince pie is

going to survive," Dad teased. "I'm licking my chops over here."

"She didn't answer. I think I'm going to walk over to the lodge and see if I can find her," Carmen said. "She must have gotten held up."

"Okay, honey," Mom said. "Here, take the pie – it's safer with you."

She wrapped the last remaining mince pie in a paper towel and gave it to Carmen. She put it delicately into her coat pocket, then headed for the door. If Joy *was* trying to avoid her, Carmen was determined not to let it happen. She couldn't leave the mountain without saying a proper goodbye, and she didn't like the idea of Joy spending Christmas night by herself, either.

She texted her just before she left the cabin, letting Joy know that she was looking for her, and then she slipped on her gloves and headed outside. The road to the lodge was quiet and cleanly plowed, and Carmen walked briskly with her hands in her pockets, gently cupping the mince pie so as not to smash it. The closer she got, she could smell the warm, inviting burning of the wood fireplaces in the lodge, and a lot of people were out on the slopes, enjoying the last remaining hours of their own vacations.

Joy was nowhere to be found in the lodge, and the girl at the front desk told Carmen that she was pretty sure Joy had clocked out about an hour ago. The stone of worry grew bigger in Carmen's stomach, and she even went out to the ski area and spent a good ten minutes staring up at the mountainside, trying to discern whether any of the little dots on the snow-covered hills was Joy. But she wasn't on the bunny slopes, of course, and Carmen wasn't ready to go looking for her on the black diamonds she preferred, so she started walking back to cabin number four.

She took out her phone on the way and removed her glove so that she could dial Joy's number one more time. Her fingers felt like ice almost immediately and she shivered as she left a message for Joy.

"Hey, it's me," Carmen said. "Please don't make me leave without getting to say goodbye to you. I know that this was doomed to be just a whirlwind vacation romance, but it feels like a lot more to me and I miss you. P.S., I have your mince pie."

She put the phone away and shivered all the way back to the cabin, feeling desolate and lonely as she walked past cabins one through three, each one lit up with strings of large, white lights along the rooflines and families enjoying their Christmases inside. Carmen thought fleetingly about hiring a car to take her into town and driving around until she could remember the street where Joy's apartment was, but she let the idea go because if Joy couldn't even answer her phone calls, then she probably wouldn't be too happy to find Carmen on her doorstep.

She found her parents curled up together on the couch when she got back to the cabin, watching the ending of *It's a Wonderful Life*. She carefully extracted the mince pie from her pocket and handed it to her dad, saying, "Here, I don't think she's coming for it."

"Oh, honey," Mom started to say, but Carmen waved her off. She didn't want the sympathy right now. She just wanted to go to sleep and stop thinking about how unexpectedly heartbroken she felt. She went down the hall to her room and closed the door softly, collapsing into the bed that still smelled faintly of Joy.

TWENTY-EIGHT

JOY

Joy left the resort as soon as she could that evening. Christmas Day was always frantic, but that night was usually one of the resort's quietest, with people settling into their cabins or their rooms to spend time with their families. She thought a lot about what her mom had said on the phone, about how she should tell Carmen how she felt about her, but in the end, she decided to stick with her original plan.

Carmen had given her one of the best holidays of her life and Joy's heart was already aching in her absence, but it didn't seem fair to go back over to the cabin and lay her emotions bare. Carmen was just a girl on vacation, a girl who had a whole other life in New York that Joy knew nothing about. It was absurd to even entertain the thought of their relationship extending beyond Christmas.

So Joy took off her elf hat – her coworker in the transportation office had been right, and she'd had to endure the merry jingling of bells on her head all day while her heart broke – and she went home.

The apartment was dark and silent, and it felt much emptier than it had just a week ago when she came home from dropping Danny off at the airport. She walked instinctively over to the light switch on the wall to turn on the Christmas tree lights, but with her finger on the switch, she couldn't make herself pretend that this was just another Christmas in Emerald Hill. She didn't want to make the apartment look festive and cheerful when her heart felt like it was twisting in on itself, so instead she went over to the couch and curled up in a soft knit blanket that her mother made for her ages ago.

She looked out the window and saw snowflakes glittering as they fell in front of the streetlight, and she allowed herself to wallow in this supremely painful moment.

Emerald Hill was a temporary kind of town, and usually Joy didn't let that get to her. Not when all her high school friends moved away, not when Mom and her new husband had to leave for the sake of her health, not when Danny got his big break. Losing Carmen hurt the most, maybe because of all the rest of the loss compounding on top of it, or maybe because...

A little voice in the back of Joy's head suggested, *Maybe because you love the rest of them, but you're in love with her.*

"That's ridiculous," Joy said out loud to the empty room, swiping angrily at a tear that had made its way to the tip of her nose.

Her phone started vibrating in the pocket of her pants, startling her out of her misery for a moment. Carmen had texted her a handful of times throughout the day, and left Joy a voicemail that she refused to listen to. It was probably her calling again, and a wave of guilt washed over Joy. She knew Carmen would be just fine once she got back to New York – she was a strong person – but Joy also knew that her cowardice must be upsetting Carmen now.

She dug the phone out of her pocket with some difficulty thanks to the folds of the blanket. She wasn't quite sure what she was going to do – reject the call and send it to voicemail so she didn't have to hear the vibrations anymore, or answer it and pour her heart out to Carmen. But when she finally got the phone free, Danny's name was on the display.

Joy shook her head a few times to try to clear the sadness from her voice, then answered with as much enthusiasm as she could muster, "Hey, Merry Christmas!"

"Merry Christmas from Ohio," he answered. "Do you have a minute?"

"Yeah, I'm off work now," Joy said. "What's up?"

"Nothing much, just wanted to call and see how your holiday was," he said. "Was it crazy at the resort?"

"As always," Joy said. "How about you? What's Christmas with The Hero's Journey like?"

"A little surreal," Danny said with a laugh. "I've never spent Christmas with a rock band before and it was shockingly normal. The front man's mom cooked us all dinner, and then we all sat around watching football."

"Weird," Joy said.

"Yeah, and you want to hear the strangest part?" Danny asked.

"Of course."

"Umm," he said, pausing for a moment, and Joy's heart leaped into her throat. She could guess what was coming, what she'd been expecting ever since she watched him walk into the airport with his guitar case at his side. "Right after dinner, they asked me to be a full member."

"That's amazing," Joy said with equal parts elation for her friend and sadness for herself. "Congratulations, Danny. You earned the hell out of it."

"Thanks," he said. "I'm still having a hard time processing it."

"You're going to be the best rhythm guitarist on the planet," she said. "And then someday you'll be lead, I know it."

"Slow down," Danny said, laughing. "One step at a time."

"So, is this effective immediately?" Joy asked.

"Yeah, I guess so," Danny said. "We're touring until the New Year, and then I guess it's back to Memphis to start working on a new album. It's crazy to say that out loud."

"So you must not be coming back to Emerald Hill any time soon," Joy said. She shouldn't have mentioned it – she didn't want to rain on her best friend's parade by reminding him how pathetic and lonely she was, but it just sort of slipped out.

"No," Danny said after a little pause. "I guess not. I might send someone to pack up some more of my clothes and my instruments, if that's okay. You can destroy the *Die Hard* poster if it makes you feel better."

Joy laughed and said, "I just might do that. I'm having a *punch Bruce Willis in the face* kind of day."

"Annoying resort guests?"

"Not exactly," Joy said, and thankfully, Danny filled in the blanks for her.

"Is this about the girl you obliterated on the slopes?"

"Yeah," Joy said, laughing at his word choice and feeling a tiny bit better. She knew there was a reason he was her best friend, despite his awful taste in popular culture and his decision to abandon her for musical fame and fortune. "She's leaving tomorrow and I think I may have fallen for her."

"Oh shit," Danny said. "That's rough."

"Yeah," Joy agreed. "We had a really nice time and I'm going to miss the hell out of her."

"I keep telling you that you've got to get out of Emerald Hill," Danny said. "Go where the people aren't so temporary."

"Yeah," Joy said. It felt like she'd heard this at least a dozen times in the past week, and it was easier advice to give than it was to follow. She couldn't just pick up her life and leave Emerald Hill the way that Danny had – she wasn't brave like that. So she did what Joy did best – she changed the subject. "Oh, by the way, my mom said she saw your concert videos on social media and she's proud of you."

"Aww," Danny said. "Tell my future mother-in-law I'm proud of her, too."

"Jerk," Joy said, rolling her eyes. "Well, I better let you get back to your lavish, rock star Christmas."

"Okay," Danny said. "Don't let yourself get too beat up about that girl. There will be others, maybe even ones who you haven't maimed."

Joy laughed again, wished Danny luck on the rest of the tour, and they hung up. She scrunched down on the couch, laying her head against the armrest, and watched the snow continue to fall outside. Danny must be right – there would be other girls – but for the moment, Joy didn't want anyone but Carmen and she couldn't imagine feeling this way about anyone else.

She glanced up at the *Die Hard* poster above the couch and thought about taking Danny up on his offer. It might be fun to get her mind off this exquisite heartbreak by brainstorming creative ways to destroy the garish, dormitory artwork that had annoyed her every single day for the last five years. But suddenly she almost liked it for reminding her of the good times she had living there with Danny, which had just officially come to an end.

DECEMBER 26

TWENTY-NINE
CARMEN

Carmen woke up the next morning to her dad sitting on the edge of her bed, nudging her out of sleep.

"Good morning," he said. "It's time to start packing to leave."

"No," Carmen whined, still mostly lost in her dreams. She'd been on the mountainside, her skis carrying her faster than she'd ever dared to go in real life, and Joy was just ahead of her, always out of reach.

"I'm sorry, kiddo," Dad said. He looked at her sympathetically and put a hand on her shoulder, and Carmen wondered if he was about to launch into some kind of fatherly speech about heartbreak – was she that transparent? But then he spared her the pain and instead said, "I wish our vacation was a little longer, too."

He got up and headed for the door, lingering there to make sure that Carmen wasn't going to fall back asleep. It reminded her of high school, when they went through this early morning negotiation almost daily. She put her thumb into the air to let him know she was awake, just like she used to, and he knocked lightly on the door frame.

"The limo's coming to pick us up in an hour and a half," he said, and then he headed into the hallway to deliver the same message to the twins.

Carmen put her hands on her eyes, rubbing away the sleep and trying to hold back the memory of last night's events. Her Christmas on Emerald Mountain had been the best one she'd ever experienced, and then it had slid like an avalanche into the worst when Joy disappeared without a trace. In the light of day, all the anguish that Carmen had felt last night at not being able to find Joy was now turning into anger. They could have had one more night together. They could have enjoyed that time, but instead Joy had left her with nothing but confusion and uncertainty.

She snatched her phone off the bedside table and checked her messages, but there was nothing other than the usual social media notifications. They'd all become meaningless to Carmen this week, and she wondered how long it would be after she returned to New York before necessity dictated that she start caring about them again. She still loved Brigid, even though it was becoming painfully obvious that they'd outgrown each other, but she had no use for a dozen updates a day about how amazing all of her friends' lives were.

She dragged herself out of bed, feeling like she could sleep until the New Year, and went down the hall to take a shower. She hoped the hot water and the steam would help clear the curious mix of melancholy and ire out of her mind, but the sight of the deep bath tub only reminded her of Joy. While she waited for the water to heat up, Carmen paced back and forth across the room and decided to give Joy one more chance to stop avoiding her before it was too late. Carmen took a deep breath and dialed Joy's number, closing her eyes as she waited.

One ring.

Two.

Three.

And then the phone connected, Joy's voice coming over the line. Carmen's heart leapt into her throat for a second before she recognized it as the same voicemail message that she'd heard last night. "This is Joy, I'm not able to come to the phone right now-"

Carmen hung up and put the phone down hard on the counter, then stepped into the shower. When she was done, she put on a pair of leggings and a sweater, then flopped her suitcase down on her bed. She chucked the phone into the bottom of it – she had no use for it if Joy was determined not to speak to her – and then she started heaping her clothes on top. She didn't care about wrinkles or keeping the dirty clothes separate from the clean ones, or even whether any of it survived the trip back to New York. She only felt supremely frustrated over the way this trip had ended. She wouldn't trade it for all the Cancun holidays in the world, but nothing this deep and meaningful could happen on the beach.

JOY

It could only be the snow, and the mountains, and Joy.

And apparently that didn't mean anything now that the trip was over.

Carmen finished throwing all of her clothes haphazardly into her suitcase and her hand was on the zipper when she saw the snow globe Joy had given her sitting on the bedside table, and she paused. Carmen picked it up and sank down on the bed, the anger draining out of her as she wondered what to do with it. It didn't feel right to take it – it belonged to Joy's dad and it should stay in her collection – but Carmen worried about leaving it in the cabin, in case it got packed up with the rest of the Christmas decorations or went into the pocket of a housekeeper.

She sighed and finished zipping up her luggage, then carried it and the snow globe out to the kitchen. She put her suitcase near the door for the driver to load into the back of the limo, then sat down at the island to wait. She shook the snow globe and set it down on the counter, watching the glittering snow fall on the little cabin and looking at the two specks on the side of the mountain that Joy had said were the two of them.

"What's that?" Maria asked on her way to the growing pile of luggage, pulling her suitcase on wheels behind her.

"Joy gave it to me," Carmen said. Maria dropped her suitcase by the door, then came and sat on the stool next to Carmen, picking up the globe and giving it another shake. She warned, "Careful."

Maria set it back down between them and said, "It's so pretty."

"Yeah," Carmen said. "I don't think I can keep it."

"Why not?" Maria asked, but before Carmen could answer, Mom and Marisol came into the room with a ruckus, lugging two suitcases each. Carmen slid off her stool and took the biggest one from Mom, helping her get it to the door.

Dad came in next, going into the kitchen and opening a bakery box in the center of the island. He took out a leftover Christmas cookie and ate half of it in a single bite, then said, "Everybody ready to go home?"

Carmen shrugged and said, "Ready as I'll ever be."

The limo pulled up soon after, loading their luggage while Dad tried to figure out how much of their Christmas feast leftovers they could bring to snack on at the airport. Carmen stood in the living room, looking at the tall, plump Christmas tree and the mountain beyond. It wasn't snowing anymore, but it had come down heavily and steadily last night and every single tree was coated in a thick layer of white. Her former self would have wanted to take a picture of this, and maybe send it to Brigid as a teaser for the amazing vacation she'd had. Carmen's phone was buried in her luggage, though, and it was better that way, with only her eyes to commit this moment to memory. When it was time to go, Dad came over and put his hand on her shoulder.

"Time heals all wounds, kiddo," he said. "Distance doesn't hurt, either."

JOY

❄

THE CASTILLOS CLIMBED into the limo and Carmen held the snow globe in her lap, the fake snow inside it moving lazily along the bottom of the scene with the motion of the car. The driver was listening to the radio, and the station he had on was still playing Christmas music.

Last Christmas, I gave you my heart. The very next day, you gave it away.

Carmen rolled her thumb over the smooth glass of the snow globe. It would be so painful to look at if she took it back to New York with her. Out of all the cheerful, optimistic songs that the DJ could have chosen, of course they were playing *that* song. She thought about the tree they'd cut down, and the turtle dove ornament that she'd chosen for Joy, wondering if she'd feel the same bitter longing when it was time to take the tree down. The limo stopped in front of the lodge so that Dad could go inside and return their key cards and settle the room service bill, and Carmen got up to go with him.

"Where are you going, honey?" Mom asked.

"I just want to stretch my legs before the drive to Denver," Carmen lied. It was easier than telling her how desperately she wanted to get the snow globe out of her possession, and much easier than sitting here and listening to sad Christmas music.

"We only just got in," Mom objected, but Carmen was already out of the limo and heading into the lodge.

Her dad was standing at the front desk and now that

Carmen was here, she wasn't quite sure what she was doing. Should she look for Joy, or just leave the snow globe at the desk for her? She joined her dad and asked, "Is Joy Turner around?"

"Not yet," the front desk attendant said. "I think her shift starts at ten today."

"What's going on, kiddo?" Dad asked, and Carmen showed him the snow globe.

"I can't leave without saying goodbye to her," Carmen said. "And I don't feel right taking this back to New York with me."

Dad glanced at the time on the clock behind the desk, then looked at her with a half-hearted smile. "I know it sucks, kid, but we don't have time to run around Emerald Hill looking for her. We've got to get into Denver for our flight."

He put his hand on her shoulder, and Carmen could feel her heart racing in her chest.

"Why don't you leave the globe at the front desk?" he suggested, turning to the attendant. "You can make sure Joy gets it, right?"

"Sure," the man said. "You can leave a note if you want."

"No," Carmen said. There were no words in the world that could sum up how she was feeling, let alone that would fit on a note scribbled on resort stationery and left at the front desk. The more her dad tried to hurry her along and get her back to the limo, the more certain she was that it wasn't just Emerald Mountain magic, or the Christmas spirit, or whatever Joy wanted to call it. What she and Joy had was more than a fling, and Carmen wasn't going to leave the resort until she was sure Joy knew how she felt. She told her dad, "I have to see her. I didn't get to say goodbye."

"We don't have time," he said.

"Dad, please," Carmen answered, and she saw Mom coming into the lobby, probably wanting to know what the holdup was and looking a little irritated at the possibility of missing their flight.

"You have her phone number, right?" Dad asked. "This doesn't have to be the last time you ever talk to her."

"She won't answer her phone," Carmen objected, and by then Mom had her by the elbow and they were leading her out of the lodge. It was with a sinking feeling that she allowed them to bring her outside, into the cold and the waiting limousine.

THIRTY

JOY

Joy woke up early on the morning after Christmas. She'd spent the night on the couch and slept fitfully, and when the sun started peeking over the mountains, she got up. She shed the knit blanket like an old layer of skin, hoping to shed the melancholy that accompanied it, but it followed her into the kitchen as she made herself a cup of tea and prepared to start her day.

There would be a lot to do at the resort today – there always was in the flux of changing seasons. The red and green Christmas decorations would start to come down, replaced by gold and silver for the New Year, and holiday guests would start to check out, Carmen among them. Life never stood still for too long in Emerald Hill, especially for the locals who were always scrambling to adapt to the changing expectations of their visitors.

Joy sipped her tea – a peppermint variety that always put her in the mind of Christmas. But she didn't want to be reminded of Christmas anymore. She hoped the New

Year would bring something better for her, something that would make the heartache she was feeling right now worthwhile, and it couldn't come soon enough for her.

She put down her mug and went over to the Christmas tree in the living room. Most years she'd keep it up until January, or until the branches started turning brown and Danny convinced her it was a fire hazard. She went to the closet and pulled out a couple of plastic bins, putting them on the floor in front of the tree as she started taking the ornaments off one at a time and packing them away. She untangled the lights and wound them into a neat circle, dropping those into the boxes as well, and last but not least, she dragged the tree out of the apartment to the curb for trash day.

When she came back inside, Joy shoved the plastic bins back into the closet beside her snowboard with the broken bindings. She would get it fixed soon because there was no way she could bring herself to use the beautiful, expensive board that Carmen had given her. Just thinking about it made tears threaten in her throat, and she pushed the thought aside.

She felt a little bit better when she stood back and looked at the empty living room. The space where the tree stood in front of the window now felt conspicuously empty and there were a few pine needs scattered on the carpet to remind her of what was missing, but she had a clear view of the bright morning sunlight and the snow on the ground outside. She took a deep breath and decided to think about that space like a blank slate. Now that Danny was gone, she could do whatever she wanted with the apartment, and now that she'd packed up Christmas, she could move on from Carmen.

Joy went into her bedroom and changed into her work clothes, then poured the remainder of her tea into a thermos to keep her warm on her drive to the resort. When she got there, it was chaos in the lobby. Her coworkers had already begun taking down the Christmas ornaments on the large tree in the entryway – the tree would stay, but the decorations would be switched to the New Year's color scheme of celebratory metallic – and quite a few families from the hotel were checking out at the front desk. Joy couldn't help scanning the crowd, looking for any member of the Castillo family, but she didn't recognize any of them and she headed for the employees-only area behind the desk to get started with her day.

Unfortunately, before she got there, someone stopped her at the desk.

"Joy," her coworker called, and she swiveled on her heel, midway through the door.

"Huh?"

"You're wanted in cabin number four," he said, and as soon as the number passed his lips, Joy felt like she might melt into the floor. Of all twenty cabins, which one could it be except that one? She'd forgotten it even *had* a number – to her, it would forever more be the Castillo cabin.

"What do they need?" she asked. She already knew it would be Carmen trying to figure out where she'd disappeared to last night, trying to pull her into that unbearable moment of saying goodbye. "If it's a room service request you can send someone else-"

"Nah," he said. "The family checked out already. I think it's a housekeeping issue."

"Oh," Joy said. "Okay, I'll go just as soon as I get clocked in."

She sighed and headed into the room behind the front desk, feeling suddenly quite peculiar. Of course there would be another family inhabiting that space shortly, or maybe a group of friends looking to ring in the New Year in lavish style. It wasn't the Castillo cabin anymore, and maybe going out there to deal with whatever problem the housekeeping staff had encountered would help Joy begin the process of forgetting. It would just be another empty cabin now.

She got herself clocked in, stored her thermos of half-drunk tea in her locker, and then went back outside. She took a few deep breaths, letting the cold air fill her lungs as she made the short walk up the road, and prepared herself for the final confirmation of Carmen's absence. She walked up the neatly shoveled sidewalk to the cabin and dug her master key out of her pocket, then let herself in.

The first thing she noticed was that the fireplace had been lit. Joy rolled her eyes and wondered exactly what kind of problem there was here if the housekeeper had time to make herself comfortable, but as she pushed the door open further and stepped into the foyer, Joy found a much more welcome sight.

"Carmen," she said, her mouth dropping open.

She was standing in the middle of the living room waiting for her, and Joy wouldn't have been more surprised if she'd had a big Christmas bow on her head. A sudden flood of relief washed over Joy and she realized how big a mistake it would have been to let Carmen go the way she almost had. Joy looked around, but the rest of the cabin appeared to be empty.

"It's just me," Carmen said, as if to answer that look. "Come in and shut the door. You're letting the cold in."

Joy did as she was told, but she lingered by the door, unsure what to do and what Carmen wanted from her. "What are you doing here? They said you checked out."

"Not exactly," Carmen said. "I couldn't leave without seeing you again."

She walked across the room, making a little detour to the kitchen island where she picked up the snow globe Joy had given her. Then she came over to where Joy was standing in the doorway, stopping only inches from her and holding the globe between them. Joy could hardly breathe with the tension building there.

Carmen gave the snow globe a little flick with her wrist, sending the glitter swirling inside it, and didn't look at Joy as she said, "I tried calling you yesterday, and I even went down to the lodge to look for you after you didn't show up last night."

"I'm sorry," Joy said. "I wanted to come, but I couldn't stop thinking about how much it would hurt to say goodbye to you. I chickened out."

"You hurt me," Carmen said. "I was so confused and

frustrated and angry. I've never felt this way about anyone before and you just disappeared."

"I'm sorry," Joy said again, and Carmen pushed the snow globe into her hands.

"I didn't think it would be right to keep this," she said. "Not if what happened this week was so inconsequential to you that you didn't even care to say goodbye to me."

"Inconsequential," Joy said, the word coming out like a yelp because it was so far from the truth. She walked over and put the snow globe down on the counter, then took Carmen's hands in hers, trying to find the right words. "I never knew I could fall for someone as fast and as hard as I fell for you. I got scared and I wanted to protect myself from the inevitability of losing you, so I put a wall up. It was the wrong way to handle it."

Carmen finally looked up at Joy, those deep, dark eyes glassy as she asked, "Were you happy to see me just now, when you came through the door?"

"Ecstatic," Joy said, and then she put her hands on Carmen's cheeks, kissing her with all of the pent-up emotion she'd been carrying around for the last twenty-four hours.

THIRTY-ONE

CARMEN

Carmen melted gratefully into Joy's lips, wrapping her arms around her and squeezing her tight so she couldn't slip away again. She was here and they were alone, and all of Carmen's frustration and sadness dissolved into pure desire. She unzipped Joy's coat and yanked it down over her shoulders, and Joy let it drop to the floor. She was kissing Carmen passionately, hungrily, and Carmen let herself be led backward into the room.

"Don't go away again," she murmured against Joy's lips, her arms around her shoulders and keeping her close.

"I won't," Joy whispered back. "I promise."

She ran her hands through Carmen's long hair and then down her neck, and then laid her down on the couch. The fire kept them warm as Joy worked quickly to undress her, lifting her up to pull her oversized sweater over her head and then laying her back down. Carmen snagged Joy by the collar of her work shirt and pulled her onto the couch, and for a moment Joy just lay there, propped up on her elbows and looking into Carmen's eyes.

Then they kissed again, and Joy's lips found Carmen's jaw, her ear, her neck. She put her hands on Carmen's breasts and her thighs against Carmen's hips, moving in the cadence of desire. Carmen closed her eyes and felt all the familiar curves of Joy's body. She'd memorized them already, and it was sweet relief to feel Joy's weight on top of her again.

She slid her hand beneath the waistband of Joy's pants, making her breathe heavier against Carmen's ear as she moved her fingers back and forth through her wetness. Joy put her head down on Carmen's chest, her hair brushing against Carmen's nose as she moved her hips in time with Carmen's hand, and then she felt Joy's fingers hooking beneath the cup of her bra, pushing it up so that her lips and her tongue could close around Carmen's nipples.

She moaned and pressed her hips up, seeking Joy, while her hand worked faster and harder between her legs. The sound echoed through the room and the heat of the fireplace coupled with Joy's lips on her skin made her whole body feel weak in the most pleasurable way.

Joy shivered against Carmen's hand, then she pulled away, throwing her shirt over her head and getting off the couch to step out of her pants. Carmen lay back, watching as Joy revealed more and more of herself, and when she was naked, she took Carmen's leggings by the waist, yanking them off her and throwing them aside. She knelt down beside the couch and kissed her stomach, then the ridge of her pubic bone, and then Carmen separated her thighs with an anticipatory, sharp intake of her breath.

Joy's lips found her again, warm and gentle, and then her tongue. Carmen felt wave after wave washing up through her body and tingling in the top of her head. Joy slid her fingers between Carmen's thighs and the sensation grew, almost too much to handle. She put her hand on Joy's hip, squeezing her, looking for a distraction, and then her fingers slipped lower, seeking her again. Carmen's breathing quickened as Joy's mouth and fingers touched her, and she moved her own hand in as much the same rhythm as she could manage, nearly out of control of her body.

With her free hand, Carmen clutched the fabric on the back of the couch, squeezing it tight as her body gave in to Joy's touch, pleasure rising inside her and overflowing into an intense orgasm. Joy joined her a moment later, putting her hand on top of Carmen's and moving her hips against her palm until she let out a yelp of pleasure and collapsed with her head on Carmen's stomach, her hand still pressed against her and feeling the spasms of her release.

"I'm glad you're still here," Joy said, still working on catching her breath, and Carmen laughed and pulled her up onto the couch. Joy put her head on Carmen's chest, where her heart was still beating fast, and wrapped her arms around her.

"Me too," Carmen said.

After a minute or two in which her heart slowed back down to normal and Joy's breathing steadied, Joy asked, "Where's your family, anyway?"

Carmen looked out the window, trying to estimate the time by the amount of light in the sky. The sun was almost reaching its peak above the mountains, and she said, "Probably still in Denver, or maybe in the air by now."

"They just left without you?" Joy asked.

"I told them that I couldn't leave here without seeing you," Carmen said. Then she made Joy sit up to look her in the eyes and said, "You changed me, Joy. I can't just go back to my old life."

THIRTY-TWO

JOY

"What does that mean?" Joy asked. She wanted to believe that it meant exactly what she was too afraid to hope for, that Carmen would stay here with her and they could be together for real – not a vacation romance or a temporary fling, but the real relationship her heart so desperately wanted. It was too much to ask for, though, so she waited for Carmen's answer and thought her heart might stop in the interim.

"I don't know," Carmen admitted with a laugh. "This is crazy, isn't it?"

"It really is," Joy said, reaching across the space between them and taking Carmen's hand. She didn't want to ask her next question, but it was necessary to figure out what their next step was. She had to know, "How long can you stay? Are we talking about a couple of hours, a day, a week?"

"I don't know," Carmen said again. She offered with a

tentative smile, "Theoretically if I bought myself a laptop, I could do all my work remotely."

Joy laughed, trying not to get herself too caught up in the promise of that statement, and said, "Isn't your family going to miss you after a couple of days? And your friends?"

"Yeah," Carmen conceded. "Probably."

"What do they think of all this?" Joy asked. Her mind was going a mile a minute, looking for all of the ways that this new development could backfire and break her heart again. She wasn't ready to be unconditionally happy about it, or optimistic about how good it felt to have this cabin all to herself with Carmen.

"My mom was kind of skeptical," Carmen admitted. "She's always been a practical type, but as soon as I decided to stay, my dad told me I had to follow my heart or live to regret it."

"Tell your dad thank you for me," Joy said, bringing Carmen's hand to her lips to kiss her fingers.

"I guess the practical answer is five days," Carmen said. "That was how long I could extend our reservation for at the cabin. Somebody else has it booked starting on New Year's Day."

"Okay. Five days is like half an eternity considering what we were able to accomplish in the last week and a half," Joy said. Carmen laughed and then in the silence that followed, Joy asked, "What do we do now?"

"Whatever we want," Carmen said, crawling into Joy's lap and throwing her arms around her.

Joy felt like her heart was welling in her chest, euphoria washing over her. She had no idea what was waiting for them at the end of the five days Carmen had given her, but it didn't matter as long as she could hold Carmen in her arms for as much of that time as possible. She wanted to shout her happiness until her voice echoed in the vaulted ceiling above them, until it reached the very mountain peaks.

Then she laughed and fell back against the couch.

"What?" Carmen asked.

"I just realized that I'm still on the clock," Joy said. She looked at the time in the kitchen – it had been over an hour since she walked over to cabin number four, and people were probably looking for her by now. She said, "I came over here because someone told me there was a housekeeping issue in this cabin."

"I know," Carmen said. "That was me. Pretty good trick, huh?"

"Yeah, it had me fooled," Joy admitted.

Carmen held Joy close and she felt every soft curve of her body. She let out a tortured moan and inhaled the intoxicating scent of Carmen's hair, her hands squeezing her hips with renewed desire. Carmen murmured into the crook of her neck, "If they ask, we'll just tell them the problem was more complicated than you anticipated. Stay a little while longer."

"You're going to get me in trouble," Joy said, but she made no move to leave. She was exactly where she wanted to be, with the girl she didn't dare to dream could be hers. "Hey, Merry Christmas, since I kind of screwed it up yesterday."

"Merry Christmas, Joy," Carmen said, wrapping her arms around her as the snow began to fall lightly outside their window.

EPILOGUE

It was a little before nine p.m. when Joy walked into cabin number four on New Year's Eve. Carmen wasn't in the living room, or the kitchen, and Joy meandered down the hallway to the bathroom, where she heard Christmas music.

Carmen was standing at the vanity and her phone on the counter beside her was filling the room with the soft, instrumental sounds of the season. She was wearing a stunning silver dress that sparkled in the light from the vanity, her dark hair shining as it cascaded down her back in meticulous ringlets, and she was leaning over the counter to apply her lipstick. Joy bit her lip as she came up behind her, wanting nothing more than to run her hands up Carmen's smooth legs and under the hem of her skirt. Carmen caught sight of her in the mirror and smiled.

"Hey," she said. "I'm almost ready."

"Take your time," Joy said, coming over and sliding

her arm around Carmen's waist. "You, this big, empty cabin, and that dress are all I need to ring in the New Year."

Carmen smiled wryly at her and said, "We're going to the party."

The resort hosted a big New Year's Eve bash every year in the resort ballroom, and the moment Joy told her about it, Carmen's eyes had lit up. There would be resort guests and Emerald Hill residents alike, with flowing champagne, dancing and a countdown at midnight. The resort even arranged to have fireworks every year, lighting up the night sky over the mountains. Most years, Joy preferred a quieter party – just her and Danny and whichever high school friends happened to be in town for the holidays – but this year she was looking forward to celebrating in style with Carmen.

They'd spent every minute of the past week together when Joy wasn't working, and even though they weren't any closer to figuring out their plans for after the holidays, Joy knew that whatever her future held, she wanted Carmen to be in it.

"Go get dressed," Carmen ordered. "I laid out your clothes in my room."

"Yes, ma'am," Joy said, leaning over to kiss Carmen's cheek before going down the hall to the bedroom.

Carmen had gone into Denver one afternoon while Joy was working to pick out her dress for the party, and she'd texted Joy to ask for her measurements, telling her that she'd found the perfect thing for her to wear. Joy tried to object, but she was quickly discovering that Carmen had a way of getting what she wanted.

Not that she had put up much of a fight – if Joy could do something to make Carmen smile, there really wasn't much question about whether or not she'd do it.

Laid neatly across Carmen's bed, Joy found a dark gray suit jacket and matching pants, along with a knit sweater vest made out of a shimmering material similar to Carmen's dress. It was soft and feminine, balanced perfectly by the sharp cut of the suit, and Carmen had done a pretty good job of finding the right size in Joy's absence. She put the outfit on and then went back into the bathroom, where Carmen was just finishing her makeup.

"You look hot," she said, raising an eyebrow appreciatively at Joy.

"So do you," Joy answered, putting her arm around Carmen's waist a second time and pulling her into a deep kiss that nearly undid all of the work she'd just done on her makeup. "Are you ready?"

"So ready," Carmen said.

❄

THEY WALKED down the short road from Carmen's cabin to the lodge and Carmen shivered with her hand in Joy's. Joy put her arm around her to try to protect her from the cold, but her dress was short and the mountain air was always colder after dark.

"Tonight's my last night in the cabin," she said while

they walked. No one else was out at this hour – all the other guests were either at the party already, or in their accommodations for the night, and Carmen was growing accustomed to this peaceful illusion of being alone with Joy on the mountain.

"Don't remind me," Joy said, kissing her and then leading her up to the door of the lodge.

"Okay," Carmen agreed. "We'll forget about if for a few more hours."

They went inside and immediately, the sounds of the party flowed over to them across the marble floors and high ceilings. The Christmas tree in the lobby had been transformed into a blue and white sparkling ode to winter, and notes of music and jovial conversation were coming from the ballroom. They checked their coats and then Joy took Carmen's hand again, leading her into the party.

The room was large and beautifully decorated, with twinkling white lights hanging from the ceiling and white garlands draped around the perimeter of the room. There were at least two hundred people there, all dressed in their finest and gathering on the dance floor and at the bar. There was a band playing on a small stage at the far end of the room, and there were floor-to-ceiling windows that took up one wall and which overlooked the snow-covered mountains.

"What do you think?" Joy asked as they headed over to the bar. "Bet it doesn't hold a candle to New Year's Eve in the Big Apple."

"New York doesn't have this view," Carmen said.

They spent a couple of hours at the party, having cocktails and dancing, and the large clock on the wall ticked closer and closer to midnight. Every time Carmen looked at Joy, she seemed even more beautiful and seductive in that crisp suit, and when she got too warm and took off the jacket, Carmen decided she couldn't take much more of this view without being able to touch her.

When the time reached a quarter past eleven, she leaned in and let her lips brush over Joy's ear as she said, "Come back to the cabin with me."

"You don't want to stick around for the countdown?" Joy asked.

"I want you all to myself when the clock strikes midnight," Carmen said, taking Joy's hand. It didn't take much convincing to get her out of the ballroom, and before long they were walking fast through the cold to get back to the solitude of cabin number four.

❄

CARMEN BEGAN UNDRESSING Joy as soon as the cabin door shut. She kicked off her shoes while Carmen carefully slid her coat over her shoulders, taking it off along with the suit jacket and hanging them both on the hook near the door. Joy turned Carmen around, pressing her hands against the wall while she unzipped her dress and let it fall to the floor. The sight was just as good as she'd imagined, the dress laying in a pool of silver around Carmen's feet and revealing a black, lacy set of lingerie.

Joy kissed Carmen's bare shoulder, putting her arms

around her from behind and pulling her close as she inhaled the scent of her hair and nuzzled into the crook of her neck.

Then Carmen turned around, pulling the vest over Joy's head and then slowly working her way down the buttons on her shirt. She never took her eyes off Joy's as she did this, a wicked little smile forming on the corner of her mouth as she got to the final button and popped it open, yanking the tails of the shirt out of Joy's pants. She tossed the shirt aside and then dropped down to her knees to undo the buckle of Joy's belt and pull her pants down. Joy stepped out of them, feeling breathless with Carmen kneeling in front of her, and then Carmen wrapped her arms around Joy's hips, putting her mouth on Joy through the thin fabric of her underwear.

She felt her legs go a little weak – she'd been anticipating this touch all evening – and she whispered urgently, "Let's go to the bedroom."

She took Carmen's hand and pulled her up from the floor, but they didn't make it far. The way Carmen's skin looked so smooth in the moonlight from the large living room window and the softness of the lace that hugged her curves tempted Joy and she pushed Carmen up against the wall, kissing her deeply. She had to have her now, touching her and tasting her.

Carmen responded with matching desire, pressing her body against Joy's and sliding her hand between her thighs to make her go weak and shivery all over again. Joy put her forehead on the wall over Carmen's shoulder and breathed heavily against her neck, panting as Carmen slipped her fingers beneath the fabric of her underwear and found her wetness. She put her hands on Carmen's breasts and moved her hips against her hand, and when she couldn't take it any longer, she pulled Carmen down to the floor.

She snagged a throw blanket and a couple of pillows off the nearby couch and arranged them into a quick little nest for the two of them, then crawled down between Carmen's knees and pulled the lace panties off. She quickly shimmied out of her own, and then Carmen was reaching for her, wanting her, needing her.

Joy let Carmen pull her hips down to meet her eager tongue, and she leaned over to stroke and rub at the tenderness between Carmen's thighs. Joy could feel her whole body trembling already, nearly losing control at the bliss of Carmen's tongue gliding over her. She slid her fingers between Carmen's thighs to the same rhythm, slowly teasing an orgasm out of her as she watched the sensation swell inside her. She wanted to capture every moment of this in her memory, the way Carmen tasted, how she smelled, how she moved beneath Joy's hand and the little, panting breaths that she took as she got closer and closer to climax.

They moved together and Joy moved her hips gently over Carmen's mouth, her thighs shaking with the effort of holding herself up when all she really wanted to do was melt into a puddle of pure ecstasy with Carmen.

They finished together, Joy collapsing on top of Carmen and lapping at her wetness as her own body convulsed and Carmen's thighs quivered around her head, and then they lay together on the floor, breathing hard and satisfied. Joy pulled the blanket around them and after a minute or two, she craned her head backward to look at the clock hanging in the kitchen.

"It's almost midnight," she said, wrapping her arms tighter around Carmen.

"So it is," Carmen said, glancing at the clock.

"Come on," Joy said, standing up and pulling Carmen to her feet. She picked up the blanket and brought it with them as she led Carmen over to the big bay windows in the living room. It wasn't quite the same view as the ballroom had, but the mountains looked majestic and beautiful from any angle.

Joy pulled Carmen into her and wrapped the blanket around them both, and they stood there for a couple of minutes, looking out at the world beyond their window. Then Carmen looked at the clock again and said, "Less than a minute now."

"Thank you," Joy said, and Carmen looked at her with a curious look.

"For what?"

"For staying," she said.

Carmen squeezed her in a tight hug and said, "I couldn't leave you."

"Good," Joy said with a contented sigh.

"You should come to New York with me," Carmen said abruptly, and it took Joy a little bit off-guard. Of course Carmen would have to check out of this cabin tomorrow to make room for a new set of guests, and they'd both have to get on with their lives at some point, but they'd done a rather admirable job of ignoring this fact while they enjoyed the extra time they got together when Carmen didn't go home after Christmas with the rest of her family.

"You really want me to?" Joy asked.

"Of course," Carmen said. "Or if not New York, then maybe we can go visit your friend the rock star, or see your mom."

"Really?"

"I can work anywhere," Carmen said with a shrug. "And I want to be wherever you are."

The sky lit up in front of them, the first of the fireworks exploding just over the ridge of the mountain. They cast the room in a bright, hopeful glow, and Joy pulled Carmen into their first kiss of the New Year. It was long and very nearly ended in them sinking to the floor again, but then she pulled away and said, "Okay. Let's do it. Let's have an adventure."

Carmen grinned widely at her, the deep pools of her eyes sparkling with the reflected light of another set of fireworks, and Joy's chest swelled with happiness. She took Carmen's hand and pulled her as fast as she could to the bedroom.

The End

❄

Also by Cara Malone

My second Christmas couple, Serenity and Liv, star in the holiday novella *Christmas in Angel Valley,* which The Lesbian Review called:

> "Sweet and gorgeous... the perfect ratio of romance, hope, and happy ending to leave us feeling jolly and light. A total shining star!"

Claim your free copy now

Printed in Great Britain
by Amazon